HOLT CLARKE

TINSEL

AND THE BOOK OF CHRISTMAS MAGIC

Cover Art and Illustrations by APRILILY21

Imagination 2 Creation Publishing

Charleston, SC USA

Books by Imagination 2 Creation Publishing may be ordered through booksellers or by contacting:

Imagination 2 Creation Publishing
www.HoltClarke.com

ISBN-13: 978-0-996979153
ISBN-10: 0996979158

DEDICATION

To Alexis, Kiera, and Luke

The inspiration behind Tinsel and the Christmas magic that has forever cast a spell over my heart.

Love you forever and always!

"…for it is good to be children sometimes,

and never better than at Christmas,

when its mighty Founder was a child himself."

~ Charles Dickens, *A Chrismas Carol*

CONTENTS

ACKNOWLEDGMENTS

The characters of Dash, Derya and the Different Ones were inspired by the many gifted children and adults on the autism spectrum. It is my hope that *Tinsel and the Book of Christmas Magic* will shine a brighter light on autism and thus a compassionate awareness of those who are often misunderstood, unfairly labeled, and ignored because they think and act differently.

I'd like to express my heartfelt gratitude to the following:

To Jackie, my ever supportive and encouraging wife who more often than I'd care to admit, pulls me out of the sinking sand of self-doubt. I'm humbled by your spiritual devotion and resilient faith. I'm blessed to be married to such an amazing woman. You're simply the best!

To my kids: Alexis, Kiera, and Luke who champion my heart and inspire my imagination.

To my illustrator, Aprilily21, for perfectly illustrating and bringing to life my vision for Tinsel along with the rest of the colorful characters and settings within the Christmas story.

And to all the readers and fans who believe in Tinsel and are eager to join her for more adventures to come.

Chapter 1

DASH

DASH IS DIFFERENT. It isn't his intention to be different. He never set out to be different. Nor did he want to be labeled different. Dash was born different. And events of late made him feel different in the worst kind of way. His world simply was not making any sense. Missing from Dash's new reality was the one person who understood him, who played with him, who made him feel safe, and who brought balance to his world. And that one person was his Dad.

"Why did you even go?" Dash asked, wearing melancholy like a cloak around his shoulders. "Mom says you've gone to the place where the angels live." Silence was the only response he received; a foreboding calm that was uncaring and absolute.

Dash felt unsafe, insecure, and unwanted. The stars were no longer aligning properly, interrupted by an intrusive black hole of loneliness and sorrow. Dash retreated to his safe place where he kept his emotions bottled up. It was what he did best. And so, to make sense of the nonsense, Dash walked along the beach looking for starfish to form a numerical pattern of a perfect 9.

Glancing down he saw several starfish scattered along the sandy seashore. Mumbling in conversation to himself, Dash began gathering the starfish. His gloomy mood was anything but the cheery kind one might expect on Christmas Eve. Dash picked up a

starfish and as if initiating a conversation with it asked, "Why are people so mean when you try to be nice and helpful?"

Continuing to walk along a familiar stretch of beach where he and his Dad often walked together, he came upon another starfish, while glancing down at it posed another troubling question. "Why do people hurt others who want to help? Makes absolutely no sense."

Bending down to pick up the starfish, Dash continued his inquisitive conversation. "And why do people hurt others just for being different?"

Several kids ran by Dash on the beach tossing sand at him as they did so. "It's the weirdo," they said scurrying off while laughing annoyingly. Dash turned away, imagining as he did, a sand bucket flying up and catching the hurtful words and burying them beneath the sand where crabs will pinch those hurtful words saying, "How does that feel? Doesn't feel so good does it?"

Being different seemed to be a bad thing like an incessant no-see-um gnat nagging about one's head on a hot summer's day. *Always out of focus and never quite where you left me.* Dash thought sullenly.

In time, the unkind voices became distant, silenced by the imaginary world that Dash often created within his mind. It was his way of drowning out those mocking voices that made fun of him. In his imaginary world, within the circle of the 9 he could control the order of events and how they would transpire without drawing unwanted attention.

Slowly, the wind began stirring, first ever so slightly, and then gaining momentum. The air was briskly cold reflecting how Dash felt inside. Upon hearing the news of his Dad's death, Dash covered himself in a cloak of melancholy. The last time Dash felt warm and happy was in the very spot he now stood. It was where he and his Dad often came to skip seashells and pebbles across the surface of the ocean. Dash always made sure that they would always stand on the beach exactly at the midway point between the lighthouse and the ocean. Those were the best of times.

Dash looked back over his shoulder for the iconic black and white Sullivan's Island Lighthouse. Looking down at this feet and then back up at the lighthouse, he adjusted by taking two steps backwards to align himself. He raised one arm while looking down it with one eye closed and the other barely open training his sight to ensure precise alignment. *"Perfect,"* Dash thought.

Dash gazed down at the spot where his Dad would've been standing. Having gathered nine starfish, Dash busied himself with meticulously constructing a perfectly formed numerical 9 out of the starfish. Standing up he stared down at the circle of the 9 starfish and allowed his thoughts to flow as freely as the wind blowing around him. He imagined his Dad standing in the circle of the nine with the tail of the 9 looping and arcing back to him.

The circle of the 9 symbolized order, safety, and security. All of which he no longer felt. Dolefully, he gazed at the sand and only saw within the circle of the 9, wet sand. Outside the circle he couldn't help but look forlornly at the impressions of his lone footprints within the sinking sand.

Dash desperately wanted to escape and soar to the stars, high above his colorless world. Closing his eyes he recalled the words his Dad once said to him, "God made you different, and that's a good thing. You're going to touch the stars. Just you wait and see."

"Different is a good thing," Dash thought opening his eyes. Little did he know how much of a good thing being different really is.

Chapter 2

THE WHISPERING WIND

THE APRICOT SUN dipped below the harbor horizon as Dash walked nostalgically along the soft sands. Gusts of salty wind stirred the loose sand along the beach. Night was settling in as the stars began to slowly awaken, stretching forth their luminous points in a celestial yawn of radiance.

The windows of several beach homes were illumined by multicolored Christmas tree lights blinking in various hues of blue, white, green, red, purple, orange, and pink. Dash stood looking on for a moment before the most pleasing smell suddenly arrested his attention. The delicious smell was coming from the opposite direction, like peppermint wind blowing in from over the ocean. Wafts of peppermint like sets of ocean waves rolled in on the wind, filling the air with the delightful smell of candy canes.

"Dash," a distant voice whispered. His heart beating a little faster, Dash cast a quick glance back over to his house thinking maybe it was his mother calling him. The only discernible movement on the porch was a gas lantern flickering by the door. Twilight was encroaching as dark shadows descended. Dash shivered at the thought of a spectral figure jumping out from behind one of the dunes.

"Dash." There it was again. Flicking his head toward movement along the dunes, he focused his attention intently upon the swaying sea oats silhouetted by the waning

sunlight. Shadows seemed to move and slither along the wind carved dunes. Rigid and still as a frog sitting on a lily pad, Dash remained fixed on the movements of the slinking shadows as his anxious thoughts began racing.

Resisting the inclination to bolt and run, Dash gazed into the circle of the 9, willing calm to his racing heartbeat. "Dash," the silvery voice called again but this time the inflection was more discernible. The pleasant sounding voice spoke in a similar calming manner that his Dad often employed to help him relax when he became unsettled. His given name is Ashton, but his Dad nicknamed him Dash because he would often run nine times around tables, trees, parked cars, you name it, as fast as he could before stopping. It was Dash's way of dealing with his frustrations and anxiety. And the faster he could restore sanity and peace, the better.

Curiosity rising, Dash gazed up and down the beach, but didn't see anyone out and about. The voice certainly was not that of his Mom's because she would first come out and sit on the porch in the rocker for nine minutes before hollering, "Dash honey, it's been nine minutes now so you come on inside."

"Who is calling my name?" Dash thought. *"And where is the voice coming from?"* It sounded as if his name was being whispered by the wind. The breeze began to intensify and eddy around him. "Dash". There it was again. Most surely it was coming from the wind and from the direction of the ocean. Dash could feel his heart pounding harder as an upwelling of fear and calm gripped him in an emotional tug of war. It was as if both contrary emotions had squared off in a duel that paralyzed him to the sand.

Movement caught his eye as something streaked overhead; a shooting star lanced across the heavens before suddenly arching around, heading straight for him. Dash was unsure whether to turn and run for safety or hold his ground and see what this bright light in the night sky was going to do. Trying to calm his rapidly beating heart, he began practicing the breathing technique his Dad taught him to help restore his calm.

"Ok, breathe in and count one, two and breathe out eight, nine," Dash thought to himself. He repeated this mantra several times as the light began intensifying as it drew closer. And then the starry heavens began twinkling in a variety of colors as if the night sky were a giant celestial Christmas tree. In rapid descent, the shooting star blazed in a silvery radiance turning dusk into dawn as it streaked ever closer.

"Dash," the voice called again. Dash was certain now where the voice was emanating from. It was coming from the shooting star. Stepping back slowly and yet keeping his eyes on the bright star, Dash found himself mesmerized by its luminous intensity. And it was blazing a cosmic trail heading straight for him.

The bright star began to shrink in size as it raced along, skimming the surface of the ocean before rushing in a torrent of gusting wind past him and slamming into a dune. Sand gushed forth into the air where it began whirling in the wind. The sand appeared to shimmer in a plethora of silver, white, and blue colors. The sheer beauty of the twirling, sandy mist inspired a sense of awe as Dash's eyes twinkled in response to the dancing elements.

The most radiant sapphire blue began glowing along the crest of the dune. And then he heard his name whispered again, "Dash". Hesitantly and apprehensively, Dash walked slowly toward the blue radiance. As the flurry of shimmering, swirling sand subsided he saw something laying in the sand. Drawing closer, he saw what looked like a book. But it wasn't just any book. It was the bluest book that Dash had ever laid his eyes upon. And it was calling his name. He had never even heard of a book that could speak, but this one certainly was.

As he drew closer, Dash found himself enveloped by the blue radiance. Looking down, his eyes beheld an ancient book made of blue leather with silver and gold accents around a stone clear as glass, that encased snowflakes and stardust swirling within. Dash knelt to take a closer look at what appeared to be miniature stars glowing in radiant hues of white and sapphire blue. A strand of silver tinsel jutted out from the side of the book shimmering like bling from rhinestones in the crescent moonlight.

Dash heard the voice again, but this time it said something different. "Discover Christmas magic on the page of the 9." The strand of silver tinsel began shimmering forming a perfect numerical pattern of a 9. The silvery voice chimed in his head again, "Discover Christmas magic on the page of the 9."

Dash couldn't resist. The ancient book was speaking his language. "Christmas hope soars in the heart!" There the voice was again calling forth from the book. Intrigued, Dash reached over and picked up the ancient book. The scent of peppermint permeated the air.

As Dash reached out and touched the silver strand of tinsel, a surge of energy charged through his body. The surge infused him with an exhilarating sensation as if he were on an accelerating roller coaster. Strangely enough, Dash felt a relaxing calm as the mysterious book put him at ease. He was curious to discover more.

Slowly opening the book, light glinted off the pages as Dash quickly lifted his hands to his eyes in an attempt to deflect the sheer brightness. As his pupils adjusted to the radiance, he peered down and saw pages white as snow with a large numerical 9 written on the right. And then the 9 darted off the page past him. Startled, Dash rocked back on his butt and began scooting and pushing back in the sand like a ghost crab scurrying as fast as he could. The area around him lit up in colors of blue and white.

What was that? Dash thought somewhat alarmed. *Or who?* The mysterious swirling dust formed a numerical 9 before morphing into the shape of a starfish. Anything that resembled a star had a hypnotic effect upon Dash. Captivated by the mysteriously whirling and entertaining dust particles he found himself relaxing and even enjoying the visual wonder. The starlight that had been coming from the dune area was now hovering above. Glancing down he watched incredulously as the mysterious book rose into the air.

And then the book began changing in essence, first changing into stardust particles and then forming into a distinct shape. Dash, frozen in wide-eyed wonder, saw unfolding before him, the most magical transformation he had ever seen.

Chapter 3

TINSEL

SNOWFLAKES SOFTLY SWIRLED off the page, appearing more blue than white, reflecting a radiant sapphire light like a bedside lamp casting its soft illumination. The strange snowy wonder increased its rotations rapidly as a form began taking shape. Transfixed and spellbound, Dash gazed in wonder at the spinning of bluish dust particles in the air. But these weren't any sort of dust particles that Dash had ever seen before, at least not when dusting his room.

Dash blinked a few times and even pinched himself to make sure he wasn't experiencing one of his daydreams that he often slips off to. Rubbing his eyes with his hands he noticed the dust particles and snowflakes along with the radiant book began coalescing into a celestial wonder. A light so brilliant and pristine formed what appeared to be…*A girl?* thought Dash incredulously. And then whirring wings appeared, arched back and humming like electricity passing through power lines. Gusts of wind blew Dash's hair back with each upward and downward swoosh of her wings.

Dash had never seen such an enchanting creature in all of his life. He gazed in wide-eyed wonder, stunned by the magical array of splendor unraveling before him. Hovering in the air with celestial wings fluttering in ethereal splendor, the young angel looked human enough, and yet her eyes sparkled like a constellation of twinkling stars.

Her hair shimmered like silver glitter. But it was her starry eyes gazing in radiance into his own that mesmerized him.

Snowflakes were falling around him although it rarely snowed where he lived. And Dash had never even heard of angels popping out of books. And had he known such, he would have spent a lot more time hanging out in the library. That was for sure.

"Hey Dash!" the delightful voice said, startling him from his rumination. The angelic girl had the most friendly smile. "I have been looking forward to meeting you?"

Caught off-guard by an actual speaking angel, Dash froze unsure how to respond. He had only seen pictures of angels, but never met one before. And he certainly hadn't heard an angel address him by name, much less his nickname. Hoping he was experiencing one of his dreams he asked, "What is your name?"

"I am Tinsel," the luminous angel said sprightly as she alighted on the sand next to Dash. Upon touching the ground, her wings softened in radiance before disappearing. Her silvery hair sparkled in the moonlight draping down just below her shoulders as a strand fell across her face perfectly accenting her brilliant silvery blue eyes.

Tinsel wore a blue outfit lined with white snow-like material on the fringes. Her outfit reminded him somewhat of a girl's version of Santa's suit but a little more trendy. Her blue top formed a v-neck with white snowy fringes accenting the top and streaking down the middle of her really cool looking jacket. Her pants were sapphire blue striped with silver accents, and fleece lined white boots.

A silver torc with a sapphire medallion at the center wrapped around her slim neck. The stone medallion appeared to harness blue fire within, refracting the light from the silver moonbeams shining down from the crescent moon. There seemed to be a peculiar interaction between the elements and the circular stone as if each were drawing from energy from the other.

"Are you an angel?" Dash asked studying her intently. Something about her looked very familiar, but he couldn't quite place it.

"You got it!" Tinsel said. But not just any angel. I'm a Christmas angel. You know, of the sort that you have seen on top of a Christmas trees."

And then it dawned on him as as he suddenly recalled where he had seen a striking resemblance. "My Dad always placed an angel at the top of our tree each year on Christmas Eve," Dash said excitedly.

"Yes he did," Tinsel said walking over with a smile. And this Christmas will be no different.

"But my Dad can't. He died," Dash said looking down sorrowfully.

"Died? Only if you allow it to be so in your mind. Death is a transition of being that brings with it a different perspective. Just you wait and see," Tinsel said with a twinkle in her eye. "Your Dad is very much alive, just not in the same form you're accustom to seeing him in. For as the mind believes, so the heart will follow."

With a tinge of hope, Dash gazed upon Tinsel's radiant smile beaming as bright as the brightest star on the darkest night. Oddly enough he felt safe with Tinsel. She had a demeanor about her that put him at ease, similar to the way his Dad could.

A silver torc materialized around Tinsel's slender neck with a translucent stone illuminating brilliant blue. Dash thought he saw the ancient book appear inside the stone before receding into a swirling mist.

"What is that?" Dash asked curisouly.

"Oh, it's a special torc or necklace as some call it. A very special torc indeed. On on each Christmas Eve I get to place it around the neck of a very special child just before departing to go on a magical adventure. The enchanted spirit stone contains within it *The Book of Christmas Magic*," Tinsel said smiling.

"*The Book of Christmas Magic*," Dash repeated to himself reflectively as he starred in awe at the fascinating torc. But his thoughts quickly turned to her words about leaving.

"Where are you going?" Dash asked not wanting her to leave.

"I am going on a magical adventure to a place where Christmas hope soars in the heart," Tinsel replied with excitement in her voice. "But I need a companion to come along to make it even more magical. Do you know of anyone that might be interested in such an adventure?"

"I'll go with you!" Dash said enthusiastically before realizing he knew absolutely nothing about flying. And the very thought of actually flying gave him the feeling of butterflies flitting about in his stomach.

Thrilled, Tinsel's angelic wings hummed to life with vibrant energy as she zipped around in the air, performing an aerial twirl before alighting back on the ground next to Dash. Her wings then dissipated before vanishing altogether.

"How do you do that?" Dash asked inquisitively.

"Land?" Tinsel asked raising her right brow.

"No. Your wings. How do you make them disappear?" Dash asked curiously walking around behind her as if searching for the vanishing wings.

"Angel wings are filled with celestial energy. We have a special ability to call forth our wings when flying around your world. Flying requires energy, so anytime I do, I just…" Tinsel's wings suddenly reappeared swooshing in upward and downward thrusts as she lifted off the ground.

"That is so cool!" Dash said becoming more comfortable in his skin around Tinsel. "Can I grow wings like you?"

"All things are possible with a little imagination and a whole lot of heart," Tinsel cackled. "But first things first," Tinsel added before unfastening the silver torc around her neck. "You will need this to fly on our journey."

"I'm going with you?" Dash asked, suddenly feeling a mixture of excitement and fear.

"You bet you are," Tinsel said beaming. "I couldn't think of anyone I would rather travel on an adventure with than you Dash!" Tinsel alighted on the sand in front of Dash and placed the magical torc around his neck. "Receive the first of several gifts on this night of hope and wonder."

Gazing into his true and unblinking eyes, she saw a pure soul with incredible potential waiting to be called forth. Admiringly she said, "Fits you perfectly. Are you ready to fly?"

"I probably should let my mom know where I'm going," Dash said responsibly, while fidgeting his shoe in the sand revealing his growing anxiety.

"I've already taken care of that," Tinsel said anticipating his response.

"Huh? You did!" Dash replied somewhat surprised.

"Sure did!" Tinsel smiled.

"What happened? Did she faint?" Dash asked with rousing curiosity as to how his mom responded.

"No silly," Tinsel said smiling and throwing back her head laughing. "I have my special ways of communicating. After all, I am an angel." She said playfully. "And besides, we will return in a moment's time as if we had never left. Trust me."

A thousand thoughts and images raced through Dash's mind. He tried to slow his thoughts down and focus on the image of the 9. He knew that being responsible in letting his mom know of his whereabouts wasn't his real hold up. It was the thought of flying. "Well, I don't have wings to fly," Dash said apprehensively.

"You don't need wings," she said hovering above the ground. "All you need to do is close your eyes and say, 'Christmas hope soars in the heart!'" Tinsel spun excitedly in the air as her wings hummed to life, eliciting a whir of snow that swirled around them.

"That's all?" Dash asked, curling his eyebrow.

"That's all! Dash you will learn soaring begins in your mind. Learn to soar in your mind and you will find yourself soaring in life. So close your eyes and imagine yourself soaring, and when you open them, let's see what happens. Give it try!" Tinsel said, inspiring belief in Dash.

So closing his eyes, Dash whispered timidly, "Christmas hope soars in the heart."

"Oh, come on," Tinsel said, provoking him to put imagination behind his words. "You can do better than that." Spinning again in the air, Tinsel whirled around him and said, "Put some oomph behind those words."

Once again and with all the enthusiasm he could muster, Dash belted out, "Christmas hope soars in the heart!"

At first he felt nothing. And then he heard a reassuring whisper in his ear, "Now open your eyes."

Chapter 4

CHRISTMAS MAGIC

THE GROUND BEGAN pulling away beneath Dash's feet. The gentle lift of the wind caused him to wobble, giving him an unsteady feeling. The stars twinkled above cheering him on in a celestial display of encouragement.

"Whoa," Dash said trying to steady himself. He darted an eye over at Tinsel, who was performing acrobatic moves in the air before arresting her movements in front of him. Her spins and twirls made him feel a bit dizzy as he desperately sought to try and steady himself.

"What if I fall?" Dash asked as if suddenly becoming aware of the possibility.

"Two possibilities will happen," Tinsel said suspended in the air next to him. "One is that I will catch you. The other is that you catch yourself."

"How do I catch myself when I'm falling?" Dash asked, trying to find his balance.

"With imagination of course," Tinsel said amusingly. "You're learning a new way of being, so think of it as riding a bike for the first time. Once you get accustomed to the new movement, the unsteadiness, the feel of the air; you will find your sense of stability, and be off and running…or in our case, off and flying."

"But if I fall, it is a lot further to the ground," Dash said flailing his hands about. Flying was unfamiliar terrority for Dash, presenting a new challenge and anxiety.

"Take hold of my hand," Tinsel said reaching out to steady him. Wobbling in midair, Dash quickly lunged, grabbing hold of Tinsel's hand as if clinging for dear life. Amazingly he felt steady, regaining a sense of balance as if standing within the circle of an aerial 9.

"Dash, you can't fall," Tinsel said reassuringly. "I won't let you. And besides, the torc around your neck gives you the special ability to fly. It's like a floating device one might use in the water. As long as you're wearing it you can fly, float, and twirl about in the air. Your imagination becomes the limit."

Releasing his hand, Tinsel spun backwards performing a somersault. "Look at you. You're still floating in the air. Now imagine that," she said giggling playfully. "Isn't this really fun?"

"Yeaahhh," Dash said with a nervous stutter, while swaying in the air, beginning to adjust to the weightlessness, acquiring a sense of balance and stability.

"It's all in your mind," Tinsel said. "See it first in your mind and then take a leap of faith. That's what Christmas magic is all about. An imaginative leap of faith that makes things happen."

Closing his eyes, Dash imagined himself soaring toward the stars. No sooner had he imagined the thought, he began feeling the rush of the cool wind in his face. Quickly opening his eyes he looked down noticing the ground rapidly retreating beneath his feet as the swaying Palm trees below rapidly began to diminish in size, looking more like grass. The multicolored lights flickering in the windows of the beach homes looked like christmassy stars illuminating the darkness below. It was all so magical.

And suddenly it dawned on Dash that he was no longer feeling afraid of falling. Soaring high above his island home below, Dash excitedly cried out, "I'm flying! I'm flying! I'm really flying!"

"Yes you are," Tinsel replied glowingly. "You really are. I never doubted you for a moment."

The world suddenly became much larger than what Dash realized. And now that he could fly, the possibilities for exploration and discovery seemed endless. Excitement began to build as Dash closed his eyes, once again imagining himself flying in a loop, while twirling around in the air. And then he did.

"Whoa," Dash said once again as he felt the rush of air and the spin of the sky above and the ground below. He felt as if he were on a Ferris Wheel going round and round. Quickly closing his eyes he imagined himself floating in the air without all the spinning. As quick as the thought itself, the world turned right side up as he slowed to a hover.

"Hey, Dash. You know you don't have to always close your eyes to use your imagination, although when distracted it's a good technique to use to block out fear. But learning to keep your eyes open while engaging your imagination is also a great way to exercise the power of your mind. Watch this," Tinsel said mischievously, as a snowball formed in her hand. And then with a wink she tossed it his way.

Dash quickly imagined a catcher's glove made of snow which formed in his hand just in time to catch the hurtling snowball.

"Well look at you!" Tinsel cackled performing a back spin. "Let's play a game. Watch what I do, and then simply imagine yourself doing the same thing. And let's see what happens."

Glancing down, Tinsel spotted several sets of waves rolling in toward the beach. "Follow my lead," Tinsel said as she streaked down toward the cresting waves, pulling up just in time to skip from the top of one wave to the next before zipping back up and twirling around like a spinning top. "Now you try it."

Wasting no time, Dash found himself zipping down enjoying the exhilarating rush of salty air rushing into his lungs. Christmas magic filled the night air.

"This is awesome!" Dash belted before arresting his descent just time to touch the top of the first wave while leaping on to the next one. After skipping along the tops of several waves, Dash swooshed upward performing a twisting aerial maneuver as the sapphire orb glowed brightly around his neck.

Dash was fully awakened to the Christmas magic, giving himself over to the power of his imagination. Tinsel flipped backwards, cackling in excitement. "Christmas magic is flowing strong in you. Now let's go see what wonders are in store on this night of nights. You ready?!"

Hovering in the air, Dash gazed down barely able to see the formation of the numerical 9 marked by the starfish on the beach. Sensing his fear of letting go of the familiar, Tinsel said, "You will find the 9 starfish exactly as you left them upon our return. I promise."

"Let's go," Dash said with a glint of adventure in his eye. "I'm ready."

Chapter 5

SOARING IN TIME

TINSEL TRACED A circle in the air with her hand. The circle in the air began to glow a brilliant white around the perimeter. With a wisp of her wings she pulled back and said, "Watch this." Taking in a deep breath, she then blew hard and the middle of the circle ignited into a dazzling blue fire with swirling snowflakes and silver stardust. Turning to look back at Dash, Tinsel said, "Through the blue fire we must go."

The swirling fire looked inviting enough, but the frightful image lurking in Dash's mind was that of being sucked into a giant vacuum hose in the sky, trapped inside a dark wet tunnel with dust particles clinging to his body. Taking a leap into the swirling beyond was taking trust to a whole new level.

"Swat that thought aside," Tinsel said playfully.

"You knew what I was thinking?" Dash asked incredulously.

"I'm an angel. I have abilities," Tinsel winked. "Don't be afraid. I will be by your side. You're looking at a travel portal. The swirling blue fire is energy created by the Christmas magic. It will not harm you, but rather transport you. And the snowflakes are just that, snowflakes," Tinsel said whimsically. "And the swirling dust particles are a blend of stardust and winter dust both of which contain creative energy."

"It's just that I've never been in a swirling blue fire before," Dash said darting his eyes.

Tinsel flew over and placed an arm around Dash's shoulders and said with a reassuring smile,. "Hey, a great mind trick to learn when feeling afraid, is to use your imagination to turn the tables on fear."

"Now look into the portal once again," Tinsel encouraged sweeping her hand toward the radiance of the blue fire.

Dash gazed intently into the swirling blue fire, feeling a tugging inside, a beckoning, a summoning that was calling forth faith and courage. Steeping into the dark corridor of his mind was a young boy with a lantern illumining everything around him. Fear like a shadowy fiend cringed while quickly darting in retreat within the escaping darkness.

"You will discover that one of your most powerful gifts is your imagination. Use it to squeeze out fear with faith. Trust in your imagination and chase away those fears," Tinsel whispered in his mind.

"Now watch this!" Tinsel said excitedly. With a swoosh, Tinsel blazed a snowy white trail into the portal vanishing beyond. With a heightened awareness of being alone, Dash envisioned fear being emboldened once again as it stalked and lurked just beyond the shadowy veil. Closing his eyes, he repeated over and over, "Christmas hope soars in the heart! Christmas hope soars in the heart! Christmas hope soars in the heart!"

A calm came over Dash as he imagined fear receding within the shadowy dark closets of his mind. Opening his eyes, he looked into the portal of swirling blue fire with renewed determination.

Suddenly Tinsel zipped back into view. "See! I'm back safe and sound and still flying. The first time trying something new is always the hardest. It's when you learn to kick off fear and strap on your faith. Believing in yourself is the most powerful kind of Christmas magic."

"I don't feel afraid anymore," Dash said becoming more confident.

"That's what makes faith so magical," Tinsel said as the blue medallion around his neck began glowing a little more brightly. "Faith let's the magic out. Think of faith as being trapped inside your mind just waiting to be unleashed. Fear often stems from bad experiences and scary thoughts that cloud your imagination with dread. But when you harness a faith-filled imagination, you unleash a very powerful magic."

Dash felt a power welling up within him. It was a strange sensation causing goosebumps to pop up along the skin of his arms. He looked up at the circle of blue fire beginning to grow brighter the braver he felt.

"Feel that sensation?" Tinsel asked. "That's courage building in you. The more courageous you feel, the brighter your faith will shine."

"It's magical," Dash said, with a smile beaming across his face.

"Yes it is! And what magic it creates. Christmas is a magical time of the year, a gift to all from Father Christmas, it just requires imagination to unwrap."

"I've never thought of Christmas time as a gift," Dash said.

"Well I bet you do now," Tinsel said as she flitted around Dash like a glowing luminary in the sky.

"Christmas is the most magical time of year," Tinsel said with a wink and a grin. "It is the season of the heart that puts the 'christstanding' in the holiday spirit."

"Chris what?" Dash said with a quizzical look on his face.

"Christstanding," Tinsel said with a cackle. "It's one of those imaginative kind of words that combines the words Christmas and outstanding. With your imagination you can also take existing words and create new words. Try it sometime. You'll be surprised what you can come up with by using your brilliant imagination."

"Christstanding," Dash said aloud. "I like the sound of that. It's what you are," he said bashfully as his cheeks blushed a rosy red.

Tinsel shot up in the air zipping and whirling round and round in excitement as she swooshed back down. Placing her arms around Dash she spun him around as they laughed and lost themselves in a magical dance amidst the backdrop of a black velvet sky illumined by multicolored sparkling stars.

"It's Christstanding!" Dash shouted excitedly as the spinning of the night sky above looked like the multicolored strobe lights above a dance floor. Off in the distance, he heard the ringing of a church bell.

The air whooshed past him enlivening his senses. Christmas magic was all around him. It was in the sight of the twinkling starry night. It was in the smell of peppermint permeating the air. It was in the ringing of the bell invoking a sense of peace on earth and good will to all. It was in Tinsel's touch as she embraced him in a magical twirl across the night sky. And it was in the snowy flurries cascading all around. It was all just so Christstanding!

Dash wanted the night to last forever. "I love Christmas time," Dash shouted.

"I know. I do too," Tinsel replied matching the excitement of his voice. "And to think we are just getting started," she said with a wink. "So what do you think? You ready to fly through this portal with me?"

No longer feeling afraid, Dash answered emphatically, "YES!"

"Then what are we waiting for? Let's go." And together they soared through the portal into the great beyond. Clinging tightly to Tinsel's hand, Dash relaxed in the moment as the most incredible vortex of white and blue light was spinning all around. Racing along an amazing trail of light that looked like a water slide in the air he just took in the thrill of the up and down rush of the movement of air as they hurtled along toward the unknown beyond.

Clinging to Tinsel's hand, Dash shouted above rushing air, "This is Christstanding!"

Tinsel glanced over at him with a beaming smile reveling in Dash's excitement. The

Christmas spirit was surging as the energy of Christmas was reaching deep into his soul and stirring to life the wonder that once fired his soul before the grief had set in. The Christmas spirit had begun working its magic in Dash.

Chapter 6

ISMUS

THE FLASHING BLUE and white tunnel in the sky slowed before vanishing altogether. Dash and Tinsel soared through a fluffy cloud bank unveiling in the distance: a coastal village, towering mountain peaks, and a few fishing boats bobbing upon an azure blue sea. A flock of seagulls was squabbling off in the distance.

Coming into view were people busy buying and selling in the local market place. Upon drawing closer, the village appeared simple without the familiar modern trappings he was used to. The clothes worn were simple and functional. There were horses, camels, and donkeys lazily walking along the dusty streets. On a nearby hillside stood an abbey with goats bleating and grazing along the hilly slope.

Looming above the coastal village was a long mountainous terrain with rock hewn tombs just above the village area. Dash and Tinsel alighted on the seashore next to a crystal clear blue sea. The panorama of strange new sights fascinated Dash. "Where are we?" Dash asked wide-eyed with curiosity.

"We have traveled back in time to the late third century, and stand upon the shores of Patara, a small coastal village within a country called Turkey," Tinsel answered.

"You mean there is a country called Turkey?" Dash asked scrunching his face.

"Yes," Tinsel laughed.

"Is this where turkeys are from?" Dash asked looking around wondering why he wasn't seeing any turkeys running around.

"No silly," Tinsel said giggling. "It's a country where the one you know as Santa Claus, grew up and is now not much older than yourself."

"This doesn't look like the North Pole," Dash said bewildered.

"That's because it's not the North Pole," Tinsel replied. "We have travelled across the Great Sea to a place far from your home and far from the North Pole."

Dash's eyes swept along the rock hewn tombs carved into the mountainside. "What are those?" Dash said pointing up at the area of the towering mountain above the coastal village.

"Those are tombs; the final resting places for those who've finished their earthly journey and now journey beyond the stars," Tinsel said.

One of the tombs began to faintly glow in colors of red and white from the inside. "Hey, did you see that?!" Dash said stimulated by the visual wonder. "That cave up there just glowed."

"It sure did," Tinsel replied amused by Dash's keen attention to details. Possessing an uncanny ability to recognize magical manifestations, he turned his attention behind him to the sounds of water splashes upon the Great Sea. The air was pregnant with the smell of salt.

A tall, slender teenage boy with dark hair and olive complexion walked along sands glistening like sun kissed gold. Stopping ever so often, he picked up a pebble before throwing it out into the Great Sea. There was something different about the teenager that Dash found intriguing, compelling him to walk in his direction. It was something about the way he seemed to gaze intently out at the blue sea.

And then Dash began noticing that the water splashes were assuming various shapes, one of which formed the perfect image of a numerical 9.

"Now, there is one whose heart soars with Christmas hope," Tinsel said as her wings quietly hummed to life. Unbeknownst to Dash, she arose in the air before fading into the waning daylight.

Dash drew closer to the water's edge in a trance-like state, intently fixated on the watery images forming over the surface: a star, a sleigh, and a shepherd's staff. Each the result of one pebble skipping along the surface. The shimmering images lingered just above the surface before falling back into the Great Sea.

"Hey, did you see that?" Dash asked realizing that his question went unanswered. Turning around, Tinsel was nowhere to be seen. Feeling alone in a foreign place, fear began creeping within the recesses of his mind.

"Tinsel!" Dash yelled out, as his heart began racing with anxiety.

"You ok?" A voice answered, startling Dash.

Turning toward the voice, Dash felt a calm come over him as the pebble-tossing stranger approached.

"I've lost a friend who was just here with me," Dash said sheepishly while looking around for Tinsel.

"Well, looks like you've found a new one," the youthful teen with merry eyes said with a beaming smile breaking across his face. "What is your name?"

Dash returned the friendly overture with a questioning look allowing an awkward silence to linger in the air.

The youthful teen with a lordly nose, swept a strand of his wiry brown hair away from his face. "Hey, you got a name?"

Jarred from his bashfulness, Dash replied flatly, "Yes."

"Well, what is it?" the smiling teen replied.

"Dash."

"Nice to meet you Dash. My name is Nicholas but everyone calls me Ismus, so as not to confuse me with my uncle who is also named Nicholas."

"Are you a fast runner?" Ismus asked.

"Not really," Dash replied. "It's just a name my Dad used to call me."

"Just a name?" Ismus replied. "If your father called you Dash then it's a special name indeed. Living into the meaning of one's name is a great responsibility. At least that's what my Dad would always tell me," Ismus said with a grin.

"I've never met someone named Ismus," Dash replied.

"Nor have I ever met someone named Dash. You see, we already share something in common," Ismus laughed lightheartedly, noticing Dash loosening up with a smile.

"Ismus!" A voice hollered from up the hillside. A burly man wearing a dark brown robe with a sash constricting his midsection was standing outside the stone abbey. "It's time to begin preparations for the Nativity Feast."

"That's my uncle Nicholas. Come on and join us for the Christmas Eve festivities!" Ismus said excitedly. "And I've got some really cool friends that I'd like for you to meet. They're crazy, but lots of fun."

Glancing around desperately trying to see if Tinsel was anywhere to be found, Dash was unsure what to do.

Noticing his apprehension, Ismus picked up a pebble and said, "Here, throw this into the sea."

Dash gave Ismus a perplexed look.

"Go on, toss it. But be sure to skip it at least three times and watch what happens," Ismus said nudging him encouragingly.

Dash drew back and sidearmed the pebble with all the energy he could muster. After skipping along the surface at least three times, a watery image of Tinsel popped up, spinning in the air before pausing to give Dash a wink and then falling back into the sea.

"Don't be afraid!" Tinsel's voice whispered in Dash's mind. "I will be watching over you." Dash's features began to soften as a relaxing calm washed over him.

"See! Your friend hasn't gone anywhere. She's just hanging out in a different form. Come on, let's go prepare for the Christmas Eve festivities!" Ismus said reassuringly. And off to Merry Abbey they went.

Chapter 7

MERRY ABBEY

UNNING UP MERRY HILL, Dash struggled to keep up, as Ismus swiftly ran up the steep hill almost effortlessly. Dash found the joyful excitement radiating from Ismus, magnetic. Reaching the front entrance of Merry Abbey, Dash paused to appreciate the large wooden doors framed by large, gray stones. The arching doors creaked upon opening, revealing lit candles in iron sconces positioned along flanking stone walls.

Passing through the narthex, they walked beneath a stone archway into a large gathering hall with vaulted ceilings. There were three rows of wooden tables running nearly the length of the great hall. Wafting in the air were delicious smells of freshly baked bread and berries, permeating throughout the hallowed space.

A teenage girl came sprinting into the great hall carrying a large platter of various clay bowls, each filled with chickpeas, lentils, olives, apricots, almonds, figs, hazelnuts, and cherries. The sprightly girl zipped to the bench before whirling the basket in a smooth fluid release as it slid across the table stopping just short of a clay bowl filled with baked bread.

"That's Blizha. She's always darting about in a hurry. A show-off if there ever was one," Ismus said jokingly.

"

Friar Nicholas walked over casting his eye upon Dash. "Who do we have here?" Friar Nicholas said with a jubiliant smile.

"Uncle, this is my friend Dash," Ismus said.

"Friend? Well, any friend of Ismus' is a friend of mine," Friar Nicholas said. "Welcome to Merry Abbey. We know no stranger here. You are most welcome at our hearth. May the light of the Christ Child shine warmly upon you on this Eve of his Nativity."

Traipsing into the great hall, was a teenage boy with a ruddy face and a tactician's nose. He had forest green eyes and carried himself with sure-footed purpose, appearing as one possessing a keen awareness, like a bird of prey surveying his surroundings. Walking alongside him was a young teenage girl with coal black shoulder length hair, gazing intently his way with chocolate brown eyes.

Strolling down the aisle of Merry Hall, it was readily apparent to Dash that she was sizing him up with her penetrating eyes. Glancing down sheepishly, Dash suddenly felt self-conscious with the limelight attention focused his way.

"Who is this?" The young girl belted, betraying no emotion.

Friar Nicholas was quick to make the introduction, "Vixie-Rae meet Dash, our new friend and guest."

"Nice to meet you Dash. You from around here. I haven't seen you before."

"No," Dash said simply, nervously stubbing his toe on the stone floor.

"Well, where are you from?" The red haired boy standing next to Vixie-Rae chimed in.

"Charleston," Dash answered.

"Never heard of it. Where is it?" The red-haired boy asked tilting his head to the side and scrunching his nose.

"South Carolina," Dash replied.

"South where?" The red headed boy asked.

"Ah, he's come to us from across the Great Sea," Friar Nicholas said. "The important thing is not where one is from, but where one is heading. We welcome our new friend, brought to us during a time such as this."

"Precisely," Ismus said with a magnetic smile. "Dash, the impetuous red haired one here is Rudimas."

Dash couldn't help but notice the dark crimson scar on Rudimas's nose. Rudimas slapped Dash on the back, "Welcome to Merry Abbey." Rubbing his stomach, Rudimas then glanced Friar Nicholas' way and asked, "When is this Nativity fast over with? This needs to be filled. I'm starved!"

"We still have much to do before ending our fast. Besides, I've not seen the Angel star shining in the evening sky as of yet," Friar Nicholas replied raising a knowing, busy eyebrow. "By the way, anyone know where Coamé, Dansar, and Praniel are? We can hardly have merriment without that trio of rogues."

"They are right behind me," a voice echoed within Merry Hall. An olive skinned teenage boy came sauntering into the room, carrying a basket of smoked fish in his arms nearly as large as himself.

"Cubyt, let me help you with that," another voice said running up behind him.

"That's ok, I've got it," Cubyt replied before leaning forward and letting the basket drop down onto the sprawling table.

Strolling in behind Cubyt was a young teenage girl with the most striking features enhanced by a winning smile. Her emerald green eyes and a straight-edged nose perfectly framed by woodsy brown hair, drew Dash in like a tractor beam.

"Coamé, did you get lost heading into the foothills earlier today?" Friar Nicholas said with a hearty laugh.

"Very funny," Coamé replied. "It finally dawned on me that you were probably sending me out to pray in the wilderness rather than find a mystery man with a haunch of lamb."

"Now why would I need to do that with one so fond of keeping her head in the clouds?" Nicholas said egging her on.

"Well, when I reach up to touch heaven I've found that heaven responds in kind. And so the task given me was not a fruitless one," Coamé quipped.

"You don't say?" Friar Nicholas added raising his right eyebrow.

Clapping both her hands in the air, Coamé turned with a bright smile as she hollered out, "Dansar and Praniel, come on in!"

Both young teenage boys strolled into Merry Hall, wheeling two open barrels with large haunches of roasted lamb jutting out from the top.

"Holy lamb chops!" Ismus exclaimed excitedly.

Coamé put a hand on her hip and held the other out toward the haunches of lamb, presenting triumphantly, her trophy catch of the day.

"Big show off!" Ismus said in playful banter.

The succulent smells of cooked meat incited hunger pangs in Dash, causing his stomach to growl. He wanted to grab one of those haunches and take a great big bite. It was all he could do to restrain himself.

"Hungry are we?" Ismus asked cackling at the rumblings of Dash's stomach.

"I could eat a whole lamb," Dash said beginning to feel at ease around his new found friends at Merry Abbey.

"Leave it to Coamé, the bringer of much joy and happiness to all," Friar Nicholas said approvingly. Everyone laughed as merriment filled the air.

Friar Nicholas stole a knowing glance at Dash standing among them strangely dressed and having journeyed from the far West. Friar Nicholas thought of the three Magi who journeyed from the far East guided by the Bethlehem star, in their search for the Christ Child. He couldn't help but think that it was no mere coincidence that Dash had found his way to them. On this night of nights, Friar Nicholas felt a stirring in his devout spirit. He believed that Dash had been divinely guided to them by the compelling allure of the Angel star.

Chapter 8

THE VILLAGE

A COPPERY SUN dipped beneath the horizon as twilight began settling upon the coastal village of Patara. The sky went through a gradual transformation as a magical blue firmament appeared, taking center stage, as evening light slowly warmed its way across the heavens. The night of nights was forming in all of its luminescent wonder.

Friar Nicholas gathered everyone together beneath a very large round window providing a sweeping view of the Great Sea. Standing with his hands on his sides, Friar Nicholas gazed up through the great hall window at the night sky, as if pondering some deep mystery.

"What is he doing?" Dash asked Ismus.

"He's watching and listening. It's the night when mystery and miracles are most prone to abound," Ismus answered with a bright-eyed look, as if eagerly anticipating an unforeseen wonder.

Coamé casually walked over next to Friar Nicholas casting her gaze to the heavens. "Has she awakened yet?" Coamé asked.

"Oh, she's awake," Friar Nicholas replied. "Of that I have no doubt."

"Uncle, I've been meaning to speak with you about something that weighs heavy

on my heart," Ismus said with compassionate concern in his voice.

"I was wondering when you would broach the subject," Friar Nicholas said turning to face his young nephew. "Is it the banished ones?"

"Fear grows in the village below and the dark shadows deepen," Ismus replied with a pensive expression. "Hope and dignity must be restored to those who have suffered long enough at the hands of bullies."

"Then let us go and do something about the cantankerous village elder and his bully sons," Rudimas said emphatically. "Why must others be cast out, simply for being different?"

"The time is soon and nigh at hand, but not just yet. Our prayers have been heard, but now is not the time to force a response prematurely," Friar Nicholas cautioned.

Rudimas started to say something, but Ismus quickly cut him off. "Then with your permission Uncle, allow Rudimas, Dash, and myself to go down to the village below and extend an invitation to the village to join us for the Nativity Feast."

Friar Nicholas looked at Dash and then to the stars above before nodding his head agreeably. "You, Rudimas and Dash may go and invite the villagers to the Nativity Feast. But exercise restraint if confronted," Friar Nicholas cautioned with a knowing glance at Rudimas.

"Come on, let's go!" Ismus said.

Dash felt fear beginning to creep down the dark corridor of his mind. Touching the medallion around his neck soothed his growing anxiety. Ismus and Rudimas darted out Merry Abbey and were clambering down Merry Hill as Dash struggled to keep up. A goat bleated from behind an olive tree momentarily spooking Dash. Scrambling down the rocky slope with pebbles sliding beneath his feet, Dash frantically caught up with Ismus and Rudimas by the time they reached the bottom of the hill.

"I was afraid I would get lost," Dash said bending over trying to catch his breath.

"Lost? Impossible to do that around here. Just look toward the Great Sea and then to Merry Hill where Merry Abbey is perched. You can't miss it. And if you still need reassurance just cling to that silver torc around your neck and you will never stray far from the light," Ismus said with a knowing wink.

Dash had the distinct impression that Ismus knew more than he was letting on. He gazed up at Merry Abbey, perched like a city set upon the hillside, noticing an otherworldly light enveloping the Abbey. For the first time, he noticed the bell tower and the gleam of the moon's pale blue light reflecting off the bell.

"Where is that light coming from? Dash asked.

"What light?" Rudimas asked.

"The white light shining over the abbey," Dash responded.

Ismus slapped Rudimas on the back and said jovially, "Why the starlight of course!"

Dash knew from the look that Ismus cast his way, that he too, had seen the celestial light enveloping Merry Abbey.

"We just built the bell tower adding the new bell this year. We shall ring it at midnight to welcome Christmas," Ismus said.

A few villagers were stirring in the streets, drawing their attention. Wearing tattered clothes, they slinked along with hollow eyes and frail faces, betraying an inner misery and an abiding hunger.

Ismus walk over to a little child barely waist high with dirt on her face and wild, unkempt hair. She was wearing a single garment that was ragged and threadbare. The way he knelt before the child and looked into her eyes demonstrated a kind and caring heart filled with compassion.

"What is your name little one?" Ismus asked reaching out to take her hand in his.

Sheepishly she remained silent and just looked down at the ground. "Where is your Mom and Dad?" Ismus asked while trying to look into her evasive eyes.

The young girl pointed up at the looming mountainside with rock hewn tombs. Dash felt a lump in his throat as he looked at the entrances of several dark tombs.

"Can you tell me your name?" Ismus asked.

"Tala," the little girl said bashfully.

"Tala, you're a brave girl," Ismus replied catching a glimmer in her eye.

"Is it Christmas time?" The little girl asked timidly.

"It most certainly is," Ismus replied with a jolly smile. "And you're invited to Merry Abbey to celebrate it with us."

A sadness came over little Tala as her eyes misted over.

"What is the matter young one?" Ismus coaxed.

"I miss my brother," Tala said as a tear trickled down her cheek.

"Where is your brother?" Ismus asked.

"The Dark Lands," Tala answered beginning to quiver.

"Move away from the girl," a menacing voice growled. "Your kind are not welcome here," the menacing voice said peering from the shadows.

"Yeah, not welcome at all!" Another grinchy voice repeated.

Spooked by the gruff voice, Tala ran off in fright. Ismus recognized the intimidating voice, as his eyebrows lowered and pinched together at the sight of little Tala scurrying away in fear. It was all he could do to restrain himself at the sound of the malevolent voice. Glancing over at Rudimas, he hoped his friend would maintain his cool as well.

Rudimas flinched in defiance and made to take a step forward before Ismus quickly rose to his feet blocking his way. "Abominus, we have come to invite the villagers to the Nativity Feast," Ismus said graciously extending the invitation, which fell on deaf ears.

"Who is the stranger?" Abominus hissed stepping into the moonbeams, revealing eyes flaming with hatred. "He wears strange clothes and looks different."

"He is a new friend who has come to us from the far West," Ismus said glancing over at Dash who was rubbing the medallion around his neck profusely.

"You speak lies! He is one of the Different Ones and is forbidden within the boundary of the village. Leave this place at once," Abominus said with a savage tone.

Abominus' towering height was readily apparent although he was concealed mostly in the darkness. Dash could discern the frame of one with broad shoulders like that of a black bear. As Abominus stepped fully into the light, Dash fearfully stepped backwards, tripping over a stone on the ground. Falling over he scrambled to get back up.

"You see," Abominus said frowning in disgust at Dash. "He possesses the look and actions of a Different One."

"Yeah, he's different," said an annoying sniveling voice hiding in the shadows.

"Still hanging out with the cursed, are we? Abominus said staring in disgust at Rudimas. "Those who associate with the Different Ones are not welcome here."

"Yeah, not welcome at all!" A grating voice echoed.

"Hey, is it possible for you to come up with an original thought?" Rudimas said to one of Abominus' bully sons, hiding behind his Dad's shadow.

Ismus quickly raised his hand to interject before matters escalated. "Abominus, we leave in peace. But know this, those who you falsely condemned and banished to the Dark Lands are children of the light. And on this night, before the tolling of the bell, the banished will celebrate among us and your deeds of darkness will be called to account."

"Well I'd be a fool's donkey if I ever allow that to happen," Abominus said in a voice tight with menace. "Be sure to convey my sentiments to your Uncle. Now leave my village!"

"Yeah, leave his village!" An echoing voice sneered.

"Let's go," Ismus said slowly backing up. "Merry Christmas, Abominus."

"Bah, hoopla!" Abominus spat, before retreating to the shadows.

Rudimas glanced over at Ismus, both surprised and heartened by his bold words.

There was a confidence about Ismus that inspired courage and hope. One thing was for certain, the die had been cast and a showdown with Abominus was inevitable.

Chapter 9

A CHRISTMAS HOPE

RETURNING TO MERRY ABBEY, Ismus, Rudimas, and Dash were greeted by a grand display of food and sweets arrayed on each of the three long wooden tables in Merry Hall. The festive atmosphere was a stark contrast to the gloom hanging over the village like a dark cloud. Merry Hall was full of life and light and the village below, nothing but fear and darkness. The contrasting realities did not sit well with Ismus.

"I can see it in your countenance," Coamé said walking up to Ismus who stood beneath the arched doorway leading into Merry Hall. "You carry the weight of the village on your shoulders. And I fear unless you put it down, you will succumb to the burden."

"How can I put it down? Especially when my waking thoughts are of those in the Dark Lands. And here of late, I've had the same recurring dream of soaring in the sky on a wooden sleigh of all things," Ismus replied with a note of melancholy in his voice.

"Where are the Dark Lands?" Dash interjected, attempting to strike up a conversation with Ismus.

"The Dark Lands are located on the far side of Merry Mountain. It is not a place you you want to find yourself after dark," Ismus said gravely.

"Who are the Different Ones?" Dash asked, recalling Abominus' unkind words.

"Not long ago, an epidemic struck our village and many died," Ismus said somberly. "Abominus lost his wife and young child to the sickness and became consumed with grief, bitterness, and hate. Believing the epidemic to be the result of a dark curse, he needed someone to pin the blame on. And so, he went after the weakest among us. He mainly targeted orphaned children who were either abandoned at an early age or whose parents died during the epidemic. Anyone else who had exhibited odd behaviors was labeled along with the orphans, 'The Different Ones'. Abominus intimidated and bullied the other villagers into supporting his firm belief that the epidemic was the work of a dark magic. And the Different Ones were banished to the Dark Lands?"

"How are they different?" Dash asked, sincerely trying to understand why Abominus had resorted to such measures.

"Some of the children felt uncomfortable around others and possessed what Abominus calls, 'shifty eyes'. Other children demonstrated obsessive preoccupation with an object, others made unusual noises, and some cowered down and flapped their arms when distressed. Some would resort to screaming when unsettled, startling villagers. Believing their odd behaviors as being the work of tormenting spirits, Abominus labeled them children of darkness, a contagion that would spread if not dealt with," Ismus said, appearing pained that such wrongful behavior was ever allowed to happen.

"Sometimes it's not easy being different, especially when it's viewed as a bad thing," Dash said, speaking as one who knew first hand the fear and hurt the Different Ones must have felt when banished from the village.

"First of all, being different is not a bad thing as Abominus would have us believe. Far from being cursed, the Different Ones are really misunderstood ones. That which he views as cursed are gifted abilities. Such is the power of imagination to see the world differently, is a perfect example of a gift," Ismus explained, becoming more excited in his reflections of those banished to the Dark Lands.

"Is using one's imagination forbidden?" Dash asked.

"Only to the extent that one's imagination differs from Abominus'," Ismus said sarcastically. "Abominus fears any thought, belief, or lifestyle that differs from his own. He and his two sons have bullied long enough. It's time we all stand up to them and do so by bringing those banished to the Dark Lands home."

"What are the Dark Lands?" Dash asked as an image of a very dark place began forming in his mind, with monsters lurking in the darkness.

"It's mostly a desert area where few people live and where roaring beasts have been known to roam. Abominus believes it is the source of the dark magic," Ismus said. "But dark magic is nothing but fear that holds the mind captive if one allows it to. Christmas magic, on the other hand, is the hope that soars in the heart, inspiring faith, imagination, and creativity. For if one loses hope, then everything begins to crumble."

"I don't understand why people fear those who are different," Dash said creasing his brows.

"People fear what they don't understand. So it's easier to avoid those that think differently, talk differently, behave differently, or believe differently," Ismus replied.

"Can the Different Ones ever return?" Dash asked.

Rudimas, who had been listening intently to the conversation, passionately chimed in, "Yes they can and soon they will, if I have anything to say about it. Abominus' superstitious nonsense has oppressed others long enough. It's time we journey to the Dark Lands and bring the Different Ones home."

Dash noticed a red scar on the tip of Rudimas' nose. "What happened to your nose?"

"He was beaten up by Abominus' two sons and a few other village bullies, for trying to prevent the banishment of the Different Ones," Ismus said glancing over at Rudimas admiringly. "Rudimas has been their strongest advocate. A fiery heart of courage burns brightly in him."

"I did what any person with a lick of common sense would've done," Rudimas replied minimizing his actions.

"You are right my red-nosed friend," Ismus said. "It is time we go and bring them home."

Coamé was standing just off to the side of Merry Abbey beneath a tree gazing into the heavens. The stars were sparkling like diamonds among the midnight velvet dome. "I've been waiting for so long to hear those words? A great light entered our world piercing the darkness on that first Christmas. How can we celebrate the Nativity Feast when the Different Ones are struggling to survive in the Dark Lands?"

Gazing up at the heavens, the stars winked down in a celestial affirmation. Nodding his head, as a mischievous smile broke across his face, Ismus said, "That settles it. I'll speak to uncle and hopefully obtain his blessing."

"We are in also," Cubyt said, walking up along with Vixie-Rae, Blizha, Praniel, and Dansar.

"Yeah, count us in," Vixie-Rae reiterated. "The absence of our friends have cast a dark shadow over this place long enough."

Knowing full well the implications of their decision, Ismus looked to Rudimas. "You are the only one to have journeyed through the dark passage and returned to tell the tale. What say you, my red-nosed friend?"

"There's still plenty of shine left in this red nose," Rudimas boasted. "Bullies and beasts are no match for the Christmas magic I sense stirring among us."

"Well then, may we all demonstrate such radiant faith," Ismus proclaimed.

After final preparations were made for the journey, Friar Nicholas provided a blessing, "May Christmas hope soar in your hearts. For you will need it on your journey. And may the light of the Christ Child shine bright upon your way."

Off in the distance, a ghost-gray mist shrouded the twin peaks of Merry Mountain.

Not to be deterred, Ismus and his merry band of Christmas companions set out for the Dark Lands, in high spirits and a desperate hope.

Chapter 10

THE DARK LANDS

THE ARDUOUS JOURNEY through the mountain passage was treacherous as a bitter wind mixed with blustering snow swirled all around. Cresting the peak of the mountain passage, Ismus gazed upon the valley below spotting several campfires flickering off in the distance. Rudimas was on scout duty scanning for any signs of danger lurking in the shadows of the mountain pass.

"Do you think our journey holds promise?" Rudimas asked Ismus.

"It must and it will," Ismus said with determination in his voice. "Fear has reigned in the village long enough. It's time to put a whole lot of merry back into Christmas."

"You really believe we can pull this off?" Rudimas said betraying a tinge of doubt.

"We must believe that we can," Ismus said with the fire of hope in his eye. "Otherwise we should turn back now. "Even if we fail this night…and we won't…our deeds shall become seeds scattered on the wind of time inspiring others to follow in our footsteps.

The stars like beacons of hope, could be seen peering through the bullying cloud breaks overhead. Off in the distance, the valley was cast in pale blue backdrop with several campfires glowing along a dark horizon.

"See!" Ismsu exclaimed. "We are not alone in our noble efforts. The starry heavens have joined our struggle. Even now the light illumines our way." The rest of their journey

was uneventful without any sight or sound from the dreadful roaring beasts.

Finally arriving, Ismus and his merry band of Christmas companions approached the camp unsure of their welcome. Their eyes were greeted by tattered tents made of sheepskin. Several of the small children were nestled together close to the flickering flames around a few scattered campfires. Only the sound of crackling and spitting flames was heard.

A foreboding feeling came over Dash as the darkness around the perimeter of the camp seemed to move. "Noticing the apprehensive look on Dash's face, Ismus said, "Don't be afraid, we are among friends."

"At least we hope, they still call us friends," Rudimas added looking around warily.

"Who goes there?" A deep voice boomed in the night.

"Do not be alarmed my friend," Ismus spoke with steady calm. "We come in peace."

The rustling of brush could be heard from behind a bush from across the camp. Stepping out of the shadow, was a tall broad shouldered man with wizened flowing hair streaked with brown and gray. Wearing a layered robe with colors of green, brown, and gray, he possessed the look of a noble wizard. Leaning upon a rowan staff, there was an air of mystery about him that captured the imagination. His wizard eyes glinted in the firelight as a breaking smile across his face conveyed a warm and welcoming presence.

"Ismus? Is that you?" The wizard called out.

Stepping into the firelight, Ismus spread wide his arms and said, "Dunder, my merry friend, it is I. And accompanying me are my stalwart companions who have also braved the treacherous journey."

Emerging from tattered tents and from the dark shadows, were the Different Ones, including small children who looked like they needed a good bath and fresh clothes. Surprised, Dash thought the Different Ones appeared perfectly normal. He had feared they would look like desert trolls; mean and frightening. But standing before him were children just like himself.

"I have missed you, my young friend," Dunder said.

"I have missed you too, Dunder!" Ismus replied heartily slapping him on the arm.

"I'm sorry I couldn't do more to save your parents," Dunder added somberly.

It was readily apparent to Ismus that Dunder had being carrying a great burden inside. "Dunder, my parents passed beyond the veil of this world and are born anew into a new world. We all shall meet again one day but our journey here is not finished. Release this burden you carry. I have made peace with their transition, as should you," Ismus said reassuringly.

Revelation settled over Dash, realizing Ismus had not only lost a parent, but both parents.

"The time of mourning has passed. My parents sojourn with the angels now. To the least of these," Ismus said with a sweep of his hands around the camp, "you're compassion honors the memory of my parents. And for that I thank you."

Suddenly a group of young boys strolled into the camp and interrupted everything. The faces didn't look friendly as the tallest among them, stepped forth with a steely coldness in his eyes. Dash began fidgeting nervously, sensing trouble.

Chapter 11

THE DREAMER

THE RUSTLING OF desert brush behind one the tents was heard, as a sarcastic voice gruffed, "Well look who has finally mustered enough courage to return."

All eyes turned to a young teen emerging from the shadows. Rudimas immediately knew who it was. Before he could reply, Coamé stepped forward and said, "Dashire, we come in peace and only desire to make right a horrible wrong."

"Right?!" Dashire spat in detest. "When I last saw you Coamé, you were praying beneath the olive tree on Merry Hill, while we were forced out of the village and banished to the Dark Lands."

"Dashire, that is enough," Dunder chastised. "Bitterness and resentment have no place here. Let us hear our friends out before we rush to judgment."

"We have all ventured to these Dark Lands, bearing hopeful hearts that we would find all of you safe and unharmed," Ismus said with utmost sensitivity, feeling the sting of Dashire's words.

"And so you have," Dashire spat with a hard look.

"What you all have had to endure since the epidemic is an unthinkable wrong, but by standing together, we can make a difference. And by so doing, ignite a beacon light of hope, expelling the darkness," Ismus said with fire of determination in his voice.

Dunder stood in deep thought for a lingering minute or so with his left hand holding firm to his rowan staff. "What do you propose?" Dunder asked with a knowing look, as if already perceiving the intentions behind Ismus' brave and heartfelt words.

"We all return to Merry Abbey together and confront the darkness that turns the heart cold," replied Ismus daringly.

"That is your proposal?!" Dashire said in great disgust. "Well isn't that mighty noble of you. Now that we have worked hard to make a life for ourselves, you trot in here as if to save the day. You're a dreamer."

"You should not be so quick to extinguish a flame before it has had a chance to burn," a steady voice said while stepping out of the shadows.

Dash looked intently around for the source of the voice before noticing a young girl with dark eyes and a smart-looking face. Several small children stepped forth as well, peering out from behind her.

"Derya," Ismus said relieved to see his friend unharmed. "It is good to see you again!"

Nodding her head slightly, Derya smiled and said, "I knew you would come and that our journey home was nigh at hand. I saw it all in a dream."

Ignoring his younger sister, Dashire noticed the red scar on Rudimas' nose, "What happened to that red nose of yours? Did Friar Nicholas paint it with lambs blood the night we were forced to leave or did you trip and fall while running scared to the safety of Merry Abbey?"

"You're wrong both times." All eyes turned to Dash who could barely believe what he had just said. Anxiously he looked to the left and right before continuing somewhat timidly, "He got the red scar from a couple of the village bullies who roughed him up for taking a stand for all of you," Dash said.

The sarcastic expression on Dashire's face turned to admiration as he looked back over to Rudimas. "Is this true?'

"Yes," Rudimas answered frankly. "And I'd like to keep it the current shade of red if it's all the same to you."

"Well why didn't you just say so to begin with. Anybody who takes a stand for us, stands with us." The tension in the air suddenly gave way to light-hearted laughter as Dashire cackled while walking over to Rudimas, giving him a pat on the back.

"The brave one who stands up to bullies. Your courageous deeds shall be recounted often and will burn brightly in the imaginations of future generations," Dunder said prophetically.

"Well, I stand a lot better on a full stomach," Rudimas replied jovially.

"But first, let us eat and be merry before we ready ourselves for the return to Merry Abbey," Ismus said signaling for the others to unload the food they had brought with them.

"Then let us eat and ready ourselves for the journey out of the Dark Lands," Dunder said with a glint of adventure in his eye.

A cheer arose from those gathered around as Ismus and his merry band of Christmas companions distributed the food.

"And who might you be, brave one?" Dashire asked, while offering a rib of lamb to Dash.

Accepting the lamb chop most eagerly, Dash replied, "I am Dash, a friend of Rudimas."

"A friend of Rudimas is a friend of mine," Dashire replied giving Dash a friendly pat on the back.

"Thank you for interrupting my impertinence and taking a stand for Rudimas. We could use more friends like you around here," Dashire said affably.

"Are you a nice friend?" Dash asked, still a bit unsure about Dashire.

"Oh, he's just the right mix of tuff huff and slappy happy!" Ismus said, clapping

Dashire on the shoulder.

"Ismus, my friend. I've missed your jolly speak," Dashire replied light-heartedly.

"Ho! Ho! Ho!" Ismus belted with a deep throaty laugh.

"What does that even mean anyway?" Dashire asked with a chuckle.

"What? Ho! Ho! Ho!" Coamé asked incredulously. "Why it's an affirmation of the Christmas spirit while making merry with kindred hearts. At least that's my interpretation," Coamé said with a wink.

"Sounds like a pretty good interpretation to me," Ismus said with a grin.

The Dark Lands didn't seem so dark anymore. Everyone sat around the crackling fire enjoying a meal together. Noticing Dash gazing up at the starry sky, Dunder leaned over and said, "Legend has it that a star is formed when the Ancient One harnesses the power of a dream and flings it to the heavens, creating a brilliant star to guide the dreamer."

Dash smiled as his thoughts turned to Tinsel and her starry wonder.

The stars shined brighter and the moonlight more radiant. It was a night when the Spirit of Christmas was stirring in a powerful way.

Chapter 12

THE IMAGINATIVE ONES

ISMUS AND DUNDER coordinated preparations for the return journey to Merry Abbey. The night was deepening with midnight quickly drawing near. A mix of emotions hung thick in the air as excitement, anticipation, and fear joined in an uneasy dance, as thoughts of the journey ahead occupied everyone's mind.

"There are about nine by my last count," Rudimas said, after making a reconnaissance of the camp. "Some don't appear able to last very long on foot. We're going to need something large enough to transport people, belongings, and provisions."

Removing a covering of thick foliage, Derya unveiled a large wooden sleigh with adjoining ropes. Dashire and several others helped haul the hefty sleigh through the unforgiving, packed snow. Slowly it groaned cutting through the unyielding, hard-packed layers of snow. "Is this large enough?" Dashire said, straining as he pulled the sleigh into the middle of the camp.

"That will do indeed," Rudimas said impressed by the size of the sleigh. "Derya is the mastermind behind the sleigh's design and creation," Dunder said, glancing over at her.

Derya smiled bashfully giving a slight nod, preferring not to be in the limelight.

"And these little guys and gals are Derya's imaginative and creative helpers," Dunder said playfully, winking at several young boys and girls who were standing next to Derya,

beaming with pride. "You know them as the Different Ones, but around here we like to think of them as the Imaginative Ones."

Stepping out from behind Derya, each child was carrying a burlap sack which they placed on the ground. With a nod from Derya, a young girl opened her sack revealing a variety of clothes made from sheep-skin. "They have been working hard for several seasons now making use of what Mother Earth provides," Dunder said proudly.

"Holy Christmas!" Ismus belted, as another child opened a bag revealing unique toys depicting various sacred symbols of Christmas whittled out of wood.

"Talk about imagination and creativity," Ismus exclaimed, considering the possibilities.

The burlap sacks were loaded onto the sleigh as the Imaginative Ones along with Derya and Dash climbed on board. Taking up positions in pairs out front of the sleigh ready to pull were: Coamé and Vixie-Rae, Cubyt and Blizha, Praniel and Dansar, Dashire and Rudimas.

Ismus and Dunder stood before the caravan. Lifting high a flaming torch, Ismus shared inspiring words to uplift everyone's spirit. "You have endured much here in the Dark Lands. Where fear once shunned you; the Spirit of Christmas embraces you. Your time in the valley of travail has come to an end."

"And may the flames from our torches join with the starlight, illuminating our way home. For tonight we shall feast with our brethren once again at Merry Abbey," Dunder said, inspiring confidence and hope.

"The night is deepening. Now let us make haste in our return to Merry Abbey while the stars smile upon us," Ismus proclaimed, giving the command to begin the long trek back to Merry Abbey.

Heaving and hauling the ropes across their shoulders, the sleigh lurched forth as a shooting star lanced across the heavens. The caravan was officially under way as spirits were high and laughter filled the air. The brilliancy of the stars danced in celestial light across the midnight blue canvas. Stars more numerous than sands on a seashore began appearing in brilliant splendor.

Dash gazed up at the heavens in starry-eyed wonder. His thoughts turned to Tinsel, *Wherever is she?* he thought to himself. *Maybe she is sitting on one of the distant stars peering down at them.* Although he couldn't see Tinsel, he knew she was close by. Of that he was certain.

All was calm, all was bright, or so it seemed. As they drew near the snow-covered mountain passage, a gathering darkness began closing in fast. Reaching a foreboding turn in the bend, Ismus waved his torch back and forth signaling for the traveling caravan to stop.

"We must continue to make haste," Dunder said to Ismus. "We can rest when we arrive at Merry Abbey."

"That's not the reason I've signaled for us to stop," Ismus said with a grave look on his face. Casting a wary eye up the steep mountain pass, Dunder spotted the shadowy creature that lurked in and out of the pale moonlight.

It was Dashire who gave voice to what everyone had silently feared, "The roaring beasts. They are upon us!"

"The roaring beast up ahead is not alone," Derya added with keen awareness of her surroundings. "There is another a hundred yards or so back. I'm not for certain, but there may be another prowling in the shadows."

And that was not all that prowled in the darkness, as dread began creeping in many hearts.

Chapter 13

THE ROARING BEASTS

A MOST TERRIFYING roar reverberated from high upon the mountain passage. The wind carried the roar amplifying the fierce savagery. "Our way across the mountain passage seems to be a bit occupied at the moment," Rudimas observed.

"Nor can we outrun the beast, for those slow of foot will be easy prey," Dashire added in a voice taut with desperation.

Dark menacing clouds circled overhead like vultures awaiting their next meal. The thick cloud-cover bullied overhead, obscuring the luminous light of the silver moon and brilliant stars. A blustery snow began to fall adding to the pall of darkness quickly enveloping the caravan.

Dunder surmised the situation with grave concern washing over his face. Ismus stood next to him straining his eyes in the darkness, trying to locate the beasts who were stealthily closing in on their current position. Everything looked bleak.

"Is that what I think it is?" Ismus asked with disbelief in his voice.

"I've long feared the Caspian tigers would return to these parts. We encountered them not long after our arrival in the Dark Lands," Dunder said grimly.

"The Caspian tiger fears nothing and no one. How did you get rid of them?" Ismus

asked, as the dawn of realization washed over him, believing it a miracle that the Different Ones survived as long as they had in the Dark Lands.

"Fear holds great sway over the imagination. And therein lies our weapon against them. For even beast that roar in the night wrestle with their own fears," Dunder said hopefully, glancing over at Derya.

All eyes turned to Derya who was placing several stones in a pattern forming a perfect circle. Dash was drawn to the circle as it began to assume the appearance of the circle within a numerical 9. Walking over, he knelt down beside Derya.

"Who is inside the circle of stones?" Dash asked.

"All of us," Derya said simply.

"And who is outside the circle?" Dash asked.

"The roaring beasts," Derya replied carefully tracing a perfect circle around the stones in the dirt with her finger.

"And what is the circle around the stones?" Dash asked processing her symbols.

"The circle around the stones is the bright glowing light that shines forth from the stones. The roaring beasts are afraid of the glowing stones," Derya said knowingly.

Having overheard their conversation, Ismus asked, "Do you know where we can find these glowing stones." Pointing to the sleigh, Derya directed his attention to a large burlap sack faintly glowing from within.

"What do we have here?" Ismus asked, walking over to the sack. Upon opening it several stones rolled out and onto the sleigh.

"I have been collecting moonstones ever since arriving in the Dark Lands. The beasts are afraid of the glowing stones," Derya said matter-of-factly.

"I see," Dunder said glancing over at Dashire who merely shrugged his shoulders, an acknowledgement of his cluelessness about the secret collection of stones that Derya had been gathering over time.

Coamé walked over to some nearby brush bending down to pick up something from the ground.

"What is that you got there?" Rudimas asked looking over Coamé's shoulder with rousing curiosity.

"A possible way out of our current fix," Coamé answered.

"So what are we going to do, throw shiny stones at the roaring beasts and hope they will scurry off?" Dashire asked in a tone dripping with sarcasm.

"This is not just any ordinary stone," Coamé replied. "It's a moonstone."

"A moonstone?" Dashire replied a bit perplexed. "Did it fall from the moon?"

"No silly," Coamé replied. "A moonstone glows when the light of the moon shines down on it."

Dunder walked over with his rowan staff in hand, "Moonstones can be found in a variety of colors such as: blue, white, red, green, purple..."

"And pink! Like the one I have in my hand," Coamé added excitedly.

The orb within the apex of Dunder's staff swirled with an emerald fire giving off an incandescent light. "Unfortunately, we need the light of the moon to ignite the the moonstones," Dunder said as if reading everyone's thoughts.

"It's great to have colorful stones and all, but how will moonstones help us in our current predicament? And besides, the moonlight is having a tough time breaking through the clouds overhead," Dashire said with frustration in his voice.

"Gather as many moonstones as you can find, but stay as close to the sleigh as possible," Ismus said with a spark of hope in his voice. Dashire looked at Ismus and then back at the darkness where several of the roaring beasts were lurking. His hesitation betrayed his fear.

"Well you heard him," Dunder said to all. "Let's gather moonstones!"

And then a break in the clouds allowed the silver moonlight to escape. Light began dancing within the moonstones as the ground lit up in bright hues of red, purple, green, pink, white, and blue.

"Holy Light!" Ismus exclaimed with eyes refracting the glowing light.

"All we need to do is place the moonstones along the sleigh rails and attach some to the pulling ropes," Derya said pulling out small little moonstone bells she and her imaginative helpers had made.

"Well, what do we have here?" Ismus said fascinated by what he was seeing and hearing. "Bells that glow!"

"They are little bells like the great bell in Merry Abbey," Derya said. "All you have to do is jingle a glowing moonstone bell and the roaring beasts will run away."

"You don't say?" Ismus said amazed at Derya's creative prowess. "Jingle bells! Now that has a nice ring to it," Ismus cracked with a hearty laugh.

Several loud roars could be heard not too far off in the distance.

"Well, you might want to start jingling some glowing bells because the roaring beasts are not exactly laughing," Dashire said anxiously.

"Ok, everyone. Listen up!" Dunder said. "Get as much extra rope as you can find and secure the moonstones all around the sleigh. Add these jingle bells along the pulling ropes and be quick about it. We must clear that mountain passage before the next wave of dark clouds obstructs the moonlight."

"And Dashire, be sure to compile a list and check off names to make sure everyone is accounted for. And check it twice. I don't want anyone left behind," Ismus added suspecting they would need a little help from above to make it back safely to Merry Abbey. And he was right.

Chapter 14

TRANSFORMED

EVERYONE HAD JUST finished placing the moonstones around the sleigh when something lurking nearby began making its way through the overgrown thicket. It was so close that Rudimas made the comment, "Sounds like a paw looking to gnaw. Ok folks, unless you can make this sleigh fly, we might need to rethink our current bright idea."

Remain in the light and you shall not fall prey to the darkness," Dunder said with a courageousness that defied fear itself.

Brooding apprehension came over Dash as he strained his eyes to see what Rudimas was hearing. A chill hung in the air like a haunting ghost, as the first of the roaring beasts stepped out and into the mountain passage ahead.

The Caspian tiger had a large furry head, glowing amber eyes, a long stocky body, powerful legs and huge paws with razor-sharp claws glistening in the moonlight. A dense coat of yellow-gold and brown stripes covered its body with yellowish white stripes streaking down its slowly swishing tail.

Things began to go from bad to worse as a second tiger stepped out from behind another thicket along the trail not far behind the sleigh. It slowly began approaching before it stopped, as if awaiting a signal to attack. Both tigers raised their heads and

remained in steely silence. There was a fierceness about their gaze that made everyone shudder in fear.

"Well, what are they waiting for?" Rudimas asked.

And then a third Caspian tiger appeared, silent as a ghost, more fearsome than the other two, powerful muscles rippling as she prowled. Its fur was white with black stripes and crystal blue eyes that shimmered like the Great Sea. The menacing white tiger fixed its cool threatening blue eyes on Ismus, waiting to pounce with coiled energy. Her stalking, crystalline blue eyes sized up the caravan, determining the easiest prey.

"Thoughts anyone?" Rudimas asked.

"Pray!" Coamé implored.

"Well, besides that," Rudimas said. "Something tells me they may not be intimidated by praying."

"I agree," Dashire added. "They may interpret our prayers as a blessing over the meal, with us being the main course."

The great white tiger let out a thunderous roar which reverberated off the towering mountainous walls. Dash looked to Ismus deriving courage from his fearlessness. The small children slinked back in fear behind the burlap sacks on the sleigh.

"We're not going to let a few roaring beasts take the merry out of Christmas," Ismus said with resolve in his voice. Walking over to the sleigh, Ismus picked up a large moonstone and returned to stand between the caravan and the great white tiger.

"We are running out of moonlight," Dashire said desperately looking overhead at the enclosing cloud layers. "There is not enough light for illumination in this snowy blizzard."

"Remember my friends, we do not journey alone. The Angel star awakens in the heavens," Ismus said facing the menacing white tiger.

"I'd really like to avoid becoming a meal to be digested in the belly of that thing,"

Dashire said, feeling more desperate by the minute.

"Then choose to digest your fear instead," Ismus replied. Dropping to one knee, Ismus raised his moonstone high above his head.

"Well, I guess that is one way to go out," Rudimas said grabbing a moonstone and joined Ismus on bended knee. Derya grabbed her moonstone joining them both on bended knee as they lifted moonstones up toward the heavens.

"You've got to be kidding me," Dashire said. "They're going to give that tiger a three course meal!"

Putting a hand on his shoulder, Dunder gently redirected Dashire's growing doubt, "When afraid of the darkness, it's smart to turn on the light."

Coamé, noticing the fear swarming around the small children on the sleigh walked over seeking to bring them comfort. She gathered them in closely and held them in a close embrace as she closed her eyes to offer a silent prayer.

At that moment, Ismus lifted his head toward the heavens and said aloud, "Behold the Light of the Angel star!" And then suddenly the thick, ominsous cloud cover above began to break apart as brilliant starlight struck the moonstone Ismus was holding. The moonstone glowed a bright pristine white. Everyone stood amazed and transfixed by the brilliancy of the white illumination.

The moonstone that Rudimas held began glowing the brightest red, illuminating the night sky with a crimson brilliance that burned brighter than a thousand campfires.

The moonstone that Derya held began glowing an emerald green adding to the white and red illuminations creating multicolored lights that lit up the night sky.

The roaring beasts scrambled away from the brilliance of the lights retreating into the shadows. Audible sighs broke out among the group as they looked toward the dark shadows with renewed hope.

But the luminous moonstones weren't the only things that were transformed. Dunder noticed the physical change that happened to Ismus. "You have strands of white hair, my young friend."

"All our hair is beginning to look white with all this white fluff falling," Ismus said with a chuckle.

"Except the white in our hair easily wipes off," Dunder demonstrated by brushing the snow off his matted hair. One of the Imaginative Ones by the name of Adalet, walked over and swept her hand through Ismus' hair and said, "The snow on your hair isn't brushing off."

"That's because it's not snow, but streaks of white hair," Derya said scooping the young girl up in her arms.

Then everyone looked over at Rudimas, as the scar on his nose had miraculously disappeared.

"Hey Rudimas, your scar is gone," Dashire said with amazement.

"Well light me up again," Rudimas said rubbing his nose.

"Hate to break up the party, but we still have a problem," Coamé said pointing to the great white tiger who had begun to move closer.

"Maybe we should circle back," Dashire said with growing apprehension.

"Going back is not an option," Ismus replied with determination. "Our way is forward."

And then the third roaring beast appeared standing next to the great white tiger. The way ahead seemed improbable. And even Ismus fought to hold at bay the encroaching doubt.

Chapter 15

UP AND AWAY

THE TIGERS BEGAN roaring in unison as their fierce eyes frighteningly refracted the light of the moonstones. The way forward seemed bleak. Snow was falling harder as the malevolent darkness seemed to fester with cruel intent.

"I'm impressed by your faith in the Light but those tigers only seem to be getting angrier by the minute," Dashire said anxiously to Ismus.

"The darkness usually does when confronted by the Light," Coamé interjected.

"Those roaring beasts are no match for the Light that burns brightest on the Eve of the Nativity," Rudimas added while walking up with a large moonstone in his arms.

The great white tiger warily stalked back and forth as Rudimas approached. "Take this," Rudimas said while heaving his moonstone which hit the ground with a thud a few feet away from the great white tiger. Shattering in pieces of luminous light, a bright red aura encircled Rudimas glowing brightest from where his scar used to be on his nose.

The great white tiger along with the other two other tigers jumped back snarling seemingly undeterred by the display of light. "The beasts seem to have conquered their fear of the light," Rudimas said.

"It appears we have a stand-off," Dunder said.

"Suggestions anyone?" Rudimas asked.

Ismus ran his hand through his snowy white hair while his companions looked to him for an answer to the current dilemma. He could see the growing desperation in their fearful eyes. Ismus was out of answers. Their only hope rested with the Angel star.

Dash began to hear the whispering wind, "Christmas hope soars in the heart." Dash looked around to see if anyone else heard it.

"Do you hear what I hear?" Dash asked Derya who was standing next to him by the sleigh.

"No, but do you see what I see?" Derya said pointing at the glowing silver torc around his neck.

"What?" Dash said looking down with eyes aglow in silver and blue light. And then he heard the whispering wind again, "Christmas hope soars in the heart!" He recognized the voice with a hopeful smile. It was Tinsel's.

The brilliance of the blue medallion around Dash's neck began intensifying. Glancing over at the white Caspian tiger staring back at him and then at the others Dash began rubbing his thumb on the blue medallion. Then the dawn of realization washed over Dash. The blue stone within his medallion was a moonstone. Gazing up at the snowy sky above, Dash closed his eyes hearing once again Tinsel's voice more clearly than ever before, "Christmas hope soars in the heart!"

Opening his eyes, Dash knew exactly what needed to be done. Dash leapt down off the sleigh and walked to the front. All eyes were now upon the strangely dressed boy from the far West.

Looking over at Derya he said, "Get the others and begin stacking everything as far back on the sleigh as you can, to create as much room as possible." Derya wasted no time complying with his instructions.

Ismus' attention was drawn to Dash and the Imaginative Ones who were busily working around the sleigh repositioning the glowing moonstones, piling burlaps sacks on top of each other while making room for more riders.

"What are they up to?" Dashire asked curiously while looking on with a bewildered expression.

"One thing is for sure," Dunder replied with a smile breaking across his face. "When Imaginative Ones put their minds to something, it usually ends up being quite creative."

"I'm not sure creativity is going to solve our current problem," Dashire said.

"Maybe they are building a tall mound for us to climb so the tigers can't get to us?" Cubyt said watching with growing interest.

"Those tigers can leap that big pile of burlap sacks in a single bound," Dashire said in frustration.

"Not if we leap them first," Dash said walking up to Dashire.

"Huh?" Dashire asked mystified.

"Recognizing the glint of Christmas magic in Dash's eyes, Ismus raised his hand signaling for everyone's silence and attention.

"And how shall we accomplish such a feat?" Ismus asked.

"Do you believe in angels?" Dash asked flatly.

"Well yes," Dashire answered, beginning to lose patience. "But how is belief in angels going to help us leap those tigers?"

"My best friend is an angel and she gave me this," Dash answered placing his hand over his heart aglow in the light of the blue medallion. "This silver torc possesses the power of Christmas magic and gives one the ability to fly like an angel. For the magic to work all you have to do is close your eyes and say..."

"Christmas hope soars in the heart!" Ismus said, finishing Dash's thoughts with a smile brimming across his face.

Walking over placing his arm around Dash. "We join our faith with yours my young friend, and together we shall conquer these roaring beasts one way or another."

"To the sleigh my merry friends. Take hold of the ropes," Ismus proclaimed while standing at the front of the sleigh, since there was no room for him to sit.

"How's that list?" Ismus asked Dunder. "Everyone accounted for?

"Yes. I've checked it twice and we're all here," Dunder answered.

Calling out to his merry band of Christmas companions, Ismus said, "To the ropes. Let's give these beasts something to roar about all the way back to the Caspian Sea."

"So how does this work exactly?" Coamé asked looking to Dash.

"Just hold tightly to the rope, and when I tell you to close your eyes, do so and don't let go," Dash answered.

Dash took his place next to Vixie-Rae and looked ahead to Rudimas positioned at the lead with crimson energy illuminating him. "Don't let go of the rope, and trust me on this, we will fly." Turning back to look at everyone else Dash added, "Hang on to the rope and cling to Christmas hope. Tinsel's magic will do the rest."

Dash closed his eyes and whispered repeatedly, "Christmas hope soars in the heart." The tigers began to roar in defiance as light began breaking free from the snowy clouds illuminating the moonstones in a variety of colorful hues. Even the snowflakes falling were shining in brilliant white light.

A beaming smile spread across Ismus' face as he gazed around at the Dark Lands that had been transformed into a winter wonderland. Belting out for all to hear, Ismus exclaimed, "We walk in the shadow of fear no longer. May the light of the blessed Christmas star shine brightly upon us all. For on this night of nights we shall soar with the angels."

"Awaiting your command," Dunder said to Ismus.

"Come now Coamé and Dashire, rise up Dansar and Praniel, onward Cubyt and Blizha, soar high Vixie-Rae and Dash. Light up the darkness Rudimas. Now, to the sky! To the sky, all!"

As one, everyone proclaimed aloud, "Christmas hope soars in the heart!" And then they pulled for all their worth, rushing headlong toward the roaring beasts. "Ho! Ho! Ho!" Ismus exclaimed as the sleigh gained lift just in time leaping over the roaring beasts.

"Only in dreams!" Dashire shouted gleefully while running on air speeding effortlessly along.

"Oh, you're not dreaming," Rudimas hollered. "We're soaring on the wind of Christmas!"

Snow was falling lightly all around Dash and the others. Closing his eyes, Dash took in the cool rush of the Christmas wind washing over him like the energy that emanates from Tinsel's wings. Although he could not see Tinsel, he felt her presence as excitement and anticipation began to swell in him like air in a balloon waiting to burst forth. Even as he was amazed at flying a sleigh with all the others, he missed Tinsel. It was after all, her Christmas magic that was enabling them to soar high in the sky over Merry Mountain.

Chapter 16

ELF OF AN IMAGINATION

EVERYTHING BEGAN TO look smaller and smaller as they all rushed forward, running on air as if gaining traction on the ground itself. The sleigh began soaring with speed, breaking through several cloud banks, breaking free to clear midnight blue skies above.

"Now this is the way to travel!" Ismus exclaimed with fascination, enjoying the miracle of flight.

"Imagination is the seed of all reality," Dunder observed, while taking in the wonders of creation below. "The Great Light imagined, spoke, and thus created. But it all begins with illumination. Creative wonders abound."

"We are soaring among the angels!" Ismus shouted while holding on tightly to the wooden handrail next to him. "This is truly a night of wonders!"

"It's just as I imagined!" Derya said with a sparkle of Christmas wonder in her eyes and markedly pointed ears.

Noticing the change in Derya's ears, Ismus said, "Hmmm, it appears that my hair was not the only thing transformed on this wondrous night. It seems the Creator has gifted you with very special ears."

"Really?!" Derya said, excitedly running her fingers along her pointy ear tips.

"I've always wanted elf ears. Elves are just so magical like the angel girl who appeared in my dream!"

"Well, now you have them. And I must say you are pretty magical yourself," Ismus said with a smile. "A most fortuitous gift from Father Christmas. Now, tell me more about this dream you had," Ismus said with rousing curiosity.

"Actually, it was more like a vision than a dream. When we first encountered the roaring beasts, not long after we arrived in the Dark Lands, we were all very scared. I closed my eyes and heard the wind whispering the words, 'Christmas hope soars in the heart.' And then I opened my eyes and saw a sleigh form in the clouds before it flew off. So I told Dunder and Dashire to build a sleigh big enough for everyone, and the time would come when we would all soar into the sky, far away from the roaring beasts below."

"Is this so?" Ismus asked Dashire, who was sitting next to him.

"She sure did. But to be honest, we did it more to appease her and to busy our minds with a task to distract our fears. I didn't think this sleigh would actually fly," Dashire said incredulously.

"A means of bringing gifts to ALL the world," Ismus said, rubbing his chin reflectively. "Now imagine that. A flying sleigh soaring like Christmas hope bringing gifts of Peace, Hope, and Joy."

"A sleigh to speed us on our way," Derya said.

"A sleigh to speed us on our way," Ismus repeated. "I like that! You certainly possess an elf of an imagination, young one. I'd love to hear more from that imaginative mind of yours."

"Elf of an imagination?" Derya replied. "Haven't heard that expression before."

"One who possesses an elf of an imagination has a special way of shaping a new reality by the power of imagination. For imagination is the seed of wonder." Ismus said, glancing up at the stars beaming brightly above.

"It's a phrase I first heard whispered on the wind the evening my parents died," Ismus continued. "I went to where my father and I often spent time together and just began skipping pebbles in the Great Sea. While pondering the movement of the ripples I remember thinking aloud, 'It would be so cool to spread Christmas cheer, like ripples going forth in all directions, bringing peace on earth and good will to all.' And then I heard the wind whisper, 'That would require an elf of an imagination.'"

"Your father was a great believer. And a jolly soul," Dunder said joining the conversation.

"That he was! I remember him saying more than once, 'A seed of Christmas hope contains within it imagination enough to create peace on earth a thrill of hope for all.'" Ismus said, gazing up at the brilliancy of the stars above.

The cool night air whipped through his hair as he closed his eyes in a gesture of silent thankfulness for their deliverance. He sensed Tinsel's presence. For it was on the Eve of the Nativity when she first appeared to Ismus, the very night his parents joined the realm of angels. Sad and distraught from the loss of both his parents, he recalled the final hope-filled words his Dad spoke to him before the light faded from his eyes. Leaving behind the most jolly smile he said, "She's coming! Oh Ismus, I can see her. She speaks softly on the wind…don't be afraid…Merry Christmas."

Stirred from his thoughts, Ismus felt a light tap on his shoulder. Derya handed him a gift carved out of wood resembling that of a reindeer bowing its head crowned with magnificent antlers, before a star above. "Merry Christmas," she said with a smile.

"Why thank you Derya!" Ismus said. "Is this what I think it is?" Ismus asked, admiring the craftsmanship of her handy work.

"It is a reindeer bowing before the Bethlehem star," Derya replied.

"Indeed it is," Ismus said studiously.

"I had a dream that I was in the North Lands where I came across a reindeer bowing before the Angel star. There were other reindeer also, and they all could fly! It was the most magical place you've ever seen where winter dust abounds. There was snow everywhere. You were in the dream also. You called the North Lands, 'The Kingdom of Christmas!' Derya said excitedly.

"You don't say," Ismus replied, taken by her enthusiasm.

"Did you know that reindeer like to paw through the snow to uncover food?" Derya asked Ismus.

"Yes. Snow shovelers of the finest sort," Ismus said merrily. "Tell me what else these reindeer can do."

"Oh, if you strap ropes to them they could pull this sleigh and soar among the stars," Derya said with a gleam of imagination twinkling in her eyes.

"Well, how would they accomplish such a feat?" Ismus asked, listening intently to Derya.

"Why with Christmas magic of course," Derya said, pointing to Dash and the others out front of the flying sleigh, "Anything is possible with Christmas magic. Just look at them."

In the distance, Merry Abbey came into view perched atop Merry Hill. The Nativity Feast was about to begin. Smiling, Ismus knew they were going to arrive just in the nick of time to join the festivities.

Chapter 17

THE NATIVITY FEAST

SEVERAL VILLAGERS STOOD on Merry Hill, gawking at the strange sight in the sky descending rapidly over Merry Mountain. Others began spilling out of the abbey, clamoring to see the spectacle in the heavens.

"What is this dark magic that descends from the heavens?" a villager asked.

"It's wind walkers sent by the Different Ones to take us all," another fearful villager yelled in fright, before sprinting off toward the Great Sea below.

Seeing the bright red glow around Rudimas, another villager cried out, "It's a fiery dragon with eighteen legs swooping down from the Dark Lands to eat us all."

Friar Nicholas gazed at the flying wonder with wide grin breaking across his face, "Saints be glorified and sinners set free!" he belted. "Ismus and his merry band of Christmas companions return to us from on high!"

Rudimas touched down first, followed by Dash and the others. The sleigh landed with a thud sending a plume of snow into the air.

"What kind of travel is this that doubting hearts see and yet struggle to believe?!" Friar Nicholas thundered joyously. Ismus leapt down from the sleigh and was swept up into a big ole bear hug by his uncle.

"Look at you," Friar Nicholas said, looking Ismus up and down seeing the strands

strands of white hair and his pale complexion. "The light of Christmas has transfigured you my nephew."

"Truly this is a night filled with mystery and awe," Friar Nicholas said, glancing over at Rudimas who possessed a red aura.

"That is the least of what has been transfigured on this night," Ismus replied.

Glancing over his shoulder, Ismus noticed the Imaginative Ones peering nervously from behind the burlap sacks on the sleigh. Sensing their anxiety, Ismus said reassuringly, "Don't be afraid. You are among friends now."

"What does transfigured mean?" Derya asked Dunder.

"It means change," Dunder answered, turning his attention warily to the gawking villagers; many of whom were murmuring amongst themselves.

In sheer surprise and delight, Friar Nicholas turned his attention to the voice he clearly recognized, "Dunder! Welcome back old friend!"

"It is good to see you again dear brother," Dunder said, giving Friar Nicholas a warm embrace, while looking over his shoulder for the one noticeably absent from among the welcoming villagers.

"Come! The Nativity feast awaits inside Merry Abbey. Let us dine as one village and celebrate Christmas together in peace and joy," Friar Nicholas proclaimed.

Walking into Merry Abbey, Ismus and his merry band of Christmas companions were greeted by the succulent smells of roasted lamb, freshly baked bread, and delicious berries. Sitting on several long wooden tables were various clay bowls filled with an assortment of chickpeas, lentils, olives, apricots, almonds, figs, hazelnuts, and cherries.

Still convinced by Abominus' dark superstitions, the majority of the villagers were wary of the Imaginative Ones and quickly filled two tables leaving no room for the returning travelers to sit with them.

With a gesture of his hand, Friar Nicholas invited Ismus and the Imaginative Ones to sit at the remaining row of tables. Clapping his hands, several boys and girls carrying clay pitchers scurried into Merry Hall and began filling the clay cups on the tables.

Raising his cup high, Friar Nicholas offered a blessing. "We welcome with humble and thankful hearts, the Christ Child into our midst. Thus we end our Nativity fast. It is with glad tidings that we welcome back into the fold our friends and family who were forced to endure who knows what kind of travails in the Dark Lands. With penitent hearts we wish to make right the wrongs done to you."

Ismus stood raising his cup in hearty affirmation as his merry band of Christmas companions stood in turn. Reluctantly standing as well, the villagers yielded to Friar Nicholas' humble example. With all cups raised, Ismus saluted with a toast, "To the Christ-child who breathes Christmas magic into the air and brings family home to join us with merriment and mirth."

The Imagination Ones began grinning from ear to ear as everyone began clanging their cups with utensils. After a blessing over the meal, everyone gave themselves to eating and drinking heartily. It was a splendid Nativity Feast. Christmas hope permeated the air as the celebratory sounds of conversation and laughter awakened the night. But all came to an abrupt halt. For the one Dunder had feared would appear suddenly did so.

Noticing the startled expressions on the faces of villagers, Ismus sensed fear lurking like a roaring beast, as everyone turned their collective attention to the entrance of Merry Abbey. Ismus knew only one who could command such fear among the villagers.

"Abominus," Friar Nicholas said with apprehension in his voice. "I am glad you have had a change of heart and decided to join us."

"Join you?" Abominus sneered. "I have not come to join you. I've come to oppose you."

"Yeah, we are here to oppose you," echoed the eldest of his two bully sons.

The villagers cringed at Abominus' seething anger. No one stirred, not even a mouse.

Chapter 18

ABOMINUS

ABOMINUS STOOD INSIDE Merry Hall, a tall, hulking man with arms thick as a tree trunk with a black flowing mane that looked like that of a black bear. Frightful black eyes accentuated a snarling face that would incite even the roaring beasts to run in fear. Standing to the left and right were his lanky sons with dark, curly hair and dirt smattered across their faces.

Rudimas made to stand to confront the village bullies, but Ismus placed a hand on his knee. "I've got this," he said with a confident wink.

"You have defied the expressed judgment of the village authority," Abominus spat while pointing his gnarly finger at Ismus. "The Different Ones are forbidden here. And neither are you or your rebellious companions."

"Abominus, you have been eating from a bowl of lava for too long," Ismus replied as chuckles broke out around Merry Hall.

"You deny the presence of dark magic that you and the Different Ones have demonstrated? Your hair is white, your skin is white, even the sound of your voice sounds different. Just look at those two," Abominus said pointing his gnarly finger at Derya and Dash.

"Yeah, just look at them," the youngest son repeated.

"He dresses strangely and her ears possess devilish protrusions," Abominus said scrunching his nose in detest. "They belong in the Dark Lands!"

"Yeah, in the Dark Lands!" The eldest son reiterated.

"And I see you continue to keep company with the foreign wizard," Abominus ridiculed, casting a wary eye at Dunder.

"You confuse Christmas magic with dark magic," Dunder countered. "Little do you know of that which you speak."

"I know enough to clearly understand that you along with those who keep company with you, are children of the dark magic," Abominus spat in disgust.

"Bitterness has made you short-sighted. Instead of accepting those gifted beyond imagining, you rejected and banished them. Your lack of vision and misguided perception leaves little room for the seed of hope to take root and grow," Dunder countered matter-of-factly.

"Dunder, you are a fool and speak with a fool's tongue," Abominus said, glaring defiantly.

"Yeah, a fool with a fool's tongue," the eldest son repeated.

"Speaking of fools," Ismus said brushing aside Abominus' bluster and his son's annoying repetition. "I believe you said…now let me see…how did you put it? Oh, yes, I remember now. You said you would 'be a fool's donkey' if you allowed the Different One's to return."

Spreading his arms out to those seated at his table, Ismus turned to Abominus with a wry grin, "Well here they are, back among us. Since you've made it fairly clear that I'm a fool, I reckon that would make you a fool's donkey."

"What are you talking about?" Abominus grumbled as a donkey's tail suddenly sprouted from his back end. While attempting to say something further, only the sound of a braying donkey came forth. Clearing his throat, he made an attempt to speak, but

once again, only the sound of a donkey braying came forth.

His eldest son tried to echo his words, but what came forth was that of a bleating goat, "Maa! Maa! Maa!" Both sons jumped and kicked while trying to reach to scratch their back end, only to feel a goat's tail jutting out. The more they bleated the quicker they changed into black haired goats with ears pointing outward.

More giggles were heard as Abominus continued turning into a black, hairy donkey with long ears. Abominus was dumbstruck by the donkey of a change coming over him, as his face began extending while adopting the hairy appearance of a donkey's head. His long legs buckled beneath him as his arms quickly changed into legs hitting the floor with a thud. Looking to his back end, Abominus saw a swishing tail. His sons were bleating profusely as short horns formed on the top of their heads.

Ismus looked over at Dunder noticing the stone in his rowan staff glowing faintly. Returning his gaze with an ironic grin and respectful nod, Dunder began tossing an apple in his hand while walking over to Abominus the donkey. "Would you like an apple?"

Abominus began braying while shaking his head side to side.

"No? Ok then," Dunder said taking a generous bite out of the apple. "Delicious! Ismus, I do believe this is one of the tastiest apples I've ever sank my teeth into. Sweet to the taste. Very good! Mmm, very good indeed." Dunder said wiping his lips giving Abominus the donkey, a wink.

"How does it feel to be different," Ismus said, somewhat amused as he gently rubbed the hairy side of Abominus' long donkey neck.. "I'm reminded of a story written in the sacred writings about a donkey who spoke with a human voice in an effort to restrain a prophet's madness. Boy, you must really have Father Christmas in a stir."

A stable hand ran into Merry Hall giving a bridle and bit to Friar Nicholas.

Abominus shook his head in a futile effort to keep the bridle and bit off his head.

"Hold on old fellow," Friar Nicholas said, while securing Abominus before handing an attached rope to Ismus.

"Take heart Abominus, we have great respect for the donkey kind and will treat you well," Ismus said pulling Abominus along toward the entrance door to Merry Abbey. At first Abominus resisted trying to bray over the bit in his mouth before giving up the fight and following Ismus outside. All those seated at the tables got up to follow the bizarre spectacle unfolding before them.

Pulling Abominus along behind him outside of Merry Abbey, Ismus led everyone to the olive tree on Merry Hill. "Abominus, my father used to say to me, 'Ismus, you're different. One day you're going to change the world.' And I believed him. Being different is not a bad thing, but a good thing. I mean, after all, you're really different now but we choose to embrace you," Ismus said giving Abominus a playful pat on his hairy donkey neck.

"So true," Rudimas said leading two goats along behind him. "You're both really different now but we choose to embrace you," he echoed with a wink.

"It's time we celebrate the magic that comes from being different. For to be different is to be colorful. So on this night of mystery and wonder, we shall welcome Christmas with the lighting of a Christmas tree!" Ismus exclaimed to all.

Chapter 19

THE CHRISTMAS TREE

ANY OF THE villagers began clamoring outside, curious as to what lighting a Christmas tree entailed. No one after all, had ever seen — much less heard of a Christmas tree.

"What is a Christmas tree, Mom?" one young girl asked.

"I think it is a tree with dried fruit on it," her mother answered, unsure herself.

"Where do Christmas trees come from?" a young boy asked his Mom.

"Why in Bethlehem where the Christ Child was born," his Mom said confident in her answer.

"How do you light a Christmas tree?" another child asked.

"With flaming torches," a father replied sagely while rubbing his beard.

Friar Nicholas hustled out of Merry Abbey to catch up with Ismus and his merry band of Christmas companions. "What is this Christmas tree you speak of, Ismus?"

"It will be one of the most colorful trees you've ever laid eyes on," Ismus replied.

"Where did you find such a colorful tree?" Friar Nicholas asked curiously.

"Oh, I didn't. Derya and the Imaginative Ones did. And they didn't find it. They imagined it," Ismus said beaming with excitement.

Ismus nodded to Derya who immediately skipped off to the large wooden sleigh

along with the Imaginative Ones. Removing several burlap sacks and a couple wooden ladders they all made their way over to the olive tree. Methodically they busied themselves with placing the moonstones all over the olive tree.

"What are the Different Ones up to?" a villager asked with growing fascination.

"Imaginative Ones," a young girl corrected.

"Why are they placing stones on the olive tree?" another villager asked.

"Yeah," another added. "Seems a bit odd to place stones on a tree."

"Those Imaginative Ones are different indeed," another villager said.

Abominus attempted to bray again but found himself flustered by the bit in his mouth.

It wasn't long before the olive tree had moonstones tied to branches all around it, at which time the Imaginative Ones stepped away from the tree. And then an uncanny silence swept over the gathered crowd. The distant stars magnified the silence as everyone looked on in anticipation.

Derya glanced over at Ismus and said, "It is finished."

Ismus turned to Friar Nicholas and said, "With your blessing, it is time to welcome Christmas with the ringing of the Merry Bell."

With a beaming smile, Friar Nicholas gave the signal, crossing himself as all gathered around did the same. Coamé then pulled on the rope attached to the Merry Bell, rhythmically ringing it with a hallowed cadence, stirring the Christmas imagination of all gathered on Merry Hill.

The stars like distant lamps were sparkling in brilliance as if winking in time with the ringing of the bell. Snow began falling and yet not a cloud hovered overhead. Something magical was stirring and Ismus sensed it.

The silver moon in all its luminous splendor held sway over the villagers who were gripped in awe and wonder. "We stand in moonlight and mystery welcoming…," Friar Nicholas began, but was unable to finish his thought as something stirred in the sky. A distant star began shining brighter and growing larger by the moment.

The moonstones, at first, began to dimly glow all over the olive tree. And then as the star in the heavens drew nearer, the moonstones began to illumine in nearly every color of the imagination.

"I've never seen a shooting star move in such a way," Friar Nicholas said with eyes transfixed on the starry wonder.

"That's not a shooting star," a voice cut in from behind. "That is Tinsel!" Dash said as his heart began pounding with excitement and delight. "She's returning!"

"Tinsel?" Friar Nicholas asked squinting up at the luminescent splendor of the approaching star.

"Yes, Tinsel!" Ismus said as a knowing smile broke across his lips. "She is a Christmas angel who shines brighter than the brightest star. It was her illumination that led kings and shepherds to Bethlehem on the night of the Christ Child's birth. She is the Bethlehem star who shines brightest on Christmas Eve."

"And how do you know this?" Friar Nicholas asked.

"Because she told me the night my father died, on the Eve of the Nativity. Her voice came to me on the whispering wind," Ismus said.

"A Christmas angel and the Bethlehem star," Friar Nicholas pondered aloud while tugging on his gray beard.

As the Angel star began drawing ever so close to the earth, the olive tree was transformed into a Christmas tree as the moonstones began to glow and sparkle like the stars in the heavens. Gasps of delight were heard by all. The children were captivated by the display of Christmas magic.

The Angel star rushed along the shore and up Merry Hill zipping past Ismus and the watching villagers toward the olive tree. The Angel star flew rapidly around the olive tree before exploding in snowy white wonder as snowflakes and winter dust showered forth over everyone.

Heaven kissed the earth in a mesmerizing display of radiant wonder on Merry Hill's hallowed ground. It was a night of magic and mystery; a night that was to become even more magical.

Chapter 20

THE ANGEL STAR

ISMUS WAS TRANSFIXED by the approaching Angel star as silver moonbeams kissed his face in celestial light. His physical transformation that had begun in the Dark Lands kindled anew, as the Angel star draw nearer. His hair became fuller and longer, as strands of silver glistened among hair of purest white. While gazing up with eyes bluer than the bluest sea, a white goatee emerged on his youthful face.

The villagers gasped at the change that came over Ismus as he assumed the look of a young monarch. Dash stared in disbelief at the physical transformation that was happening to Ismus.

Kneeling down on bended knee, Ismua bowed his head in reverence before the approaching Angel star. The villagers quickly followed suit, dropping to their knees while crossing themselves as they did so. They had lived long under the terrible rule of fear. And now a peace was born anew in them, as all welcomed with thankful hearts, the descent of Christmas hope, in the persona of an angel.

Gazing to the heavens in spiritual devotion, Friar Nicholas began quoting from the sacred writings, "Glory to God in the highest heaven, and on earth peace to those on whom his favor rests."

Raising his head, Ismus began to sing a Christmas carol. Upon repeating the carol,

the villagers joined in the chorus, voices blending in harmonious accord as the stars above twinkled in joyful delight. It was an enchanting time as fear was was dispelled and shivering bodies thawed by the heartwarming song.

Shine down on us angel star,

Bring to us your light from afar.

Captured by your blessed gaze,

We are thus set free from our worldly craze.

Lift us to yonder light,

May it in us glow ever bright.

Guide us to heaven's child,

Who awaits us ever meek and mild.

Derya and the Imaginative Ones watched in awe as the Angel star soared down, streaking across the Great Sea. Fine dust powdered the air like a lightly veiled mist that fell magically all around. The sound of the whispering wind echoing Ismus' Christmas carol could be heard.

Dash's attention was diverted by a familiar voice whispering to him in the wind. Trying to locate the source of the sound, he glanced up at the rock hewn tomb in the mountain above the village. The tomb was illumined by a bright white glow with two silhouetted figures standing at the entrance.

A rush of wind reclaimed Dash's attention as the Angel star whooshed past him toward the olive tree. Circling the the olive tree in rapid succession, the Angel star exploded in snowy white wonder as snowflakes showered forth.

"Look up there!" a child yelled in glee.

All eyes immediately turned to the source of the child's fascination. And there she sat.

Perched high atop the olive tree, that was now brightly lit in a variety of colors, was none other than Tinsel.

"It's a girl!" one villager exclaimed. "How did she get up there?"

"It's one of the Imaginative Ones," another villager said. '

"No, it's the Angel star," Derya said eyes aglow with starry fascination.

"An angel doesn't dress like that," another villager said. "They all dress in white robes."

"It's the dark magic!" another villager exclaimed fearfully.

"Merry Christmas!" Tinsel said. Shocked by her words, several villagers fainted from fright as if she had said, "Boo!" Others just stood speechless, mesmerized by her colorful appearance and the sound of her voice that held them enraptured.

Tinsel's silver hair shimmered in the moonlight. Her blue eyes sparkled like moonbeams dancing on the Great Sea. But it was her clothes that made a fashion impression beyond even Derya's wildest imagination. "She is the most beautiful Christmas angel ever," Derya said.

A celestial sensation, Tinsel wore a sapphire blue floppy cone cap with a white bobble on top and white fleece around the crown with shimmering silver hair dropping to her shoulders. Her suit was sapphire blue with white fleece fringes on the sleeves, top, and skirt with silver accents that looked like swirls of snow. She wore striped white and sapphire blue stockings with white boots and white fleece fringes around the top.

"Now that's what I call dressmas," Derya said admiring Tinsel's Christmas outfit. Derya leaned over to Ismus and whispered, "Now that's an imaginative outfit." They exchanged a knowing glance as thoughts of Christmas future swirled in their Christmassy imaginations.

Tinsel leapt with a twirl from the top of the Christmas tree as her ethereal wings sprang to life humming with energy. She alighted on the ground before Ismus as the energy of her angelic wings dissipated and vanished.

Ismus nodded his head in respect. Tinsel did a slight curtsy in response, giggling as she did so. Wasting no time, Dash ran up and gave Tinsel a tight, lingering hug.

"It's good to see you again as well," Tinsel said happily.

"I knew you would return!" Dash said sounding relieved that his faith in her reappearance was realized.

"And you have never been more right," Tinsel replied with a smile. "I've kept my starry eye on you and I must say how impressed I am with your gifted imagination. It has served you and others well."

Tinsel cast her starry gaze over at Derya and all those who had lived as outcasts in the Dark Lands. She could see the insecurity and uncertainty in some of their eyes as they fidgeted and shuffled their feet nervously. They were struggling with whether she would accept them.

Tinsel's wings sprung to life in humming energy as she leapt forth into the air before alighting by the sleigh. "And to you," she said. "You are Heaven's champions. Courageously and heroically you made your way in the Dark Lands. You never stopped believing in your imagination. And look at what your imaginative creativity has made possible," Tinsel said pointing at the Christmas tree, the sleigh, and all those gathered around Merry Hill.

"You are champions of imagination and your deeds shall be sung by prophets and bards for ages to come. Keep believing in your dreams, for dreamers succeed when they believe in their imagination," Tinsel proclaimed. She then placed around each of them a shimmering silver necklace medallion encasing a small sapphire moonstone. Smiling with delight, each of their faces beamed as bright as a Christmas Tree.

After receiving her necklace, Derya walked over and adorned the Christmas tree with it. And then the other Imaginative Ones followed her example decorating the Christmas tree with their necklace medallions, providing the very first Christmas tree ornaments.

Tinsel beamed in admiration at the exemplary character and commendable conduct of Derya and the Imaginative Ones. Their actions would serve as the precursor for the rise of the Christmas elves who would play an important role in the spreading of Christmas magic to the hearts and minds of children all around the world.

Chapter 21

SANTA CLAUS

APPEARING ACROSS THE top of Merry Mountain were Christmas angels dressed in various colors of red, white, gold, silver, blue, green, and purple; as colorful as the moonstones sparkling on the Christmas tree. Wings aglow in resplendent colors coursing with energy, fanned out behind them.

"Unto us the angels descend," Friar Nicholas said beholding the majestic angels.

Seeing the angels lined atop Merry Mountain caused many of the villagers to tremble in fear. Sensing their fear Tinsel said, "Do not be afraid. They are Christmas angels who have gathered to celebrate the coronation of one among you. Please rise."
Everyone stood to their feet as Tinsel approached Ismus and said cheerfully, "For among you, one is chosen to bear the Scepter of Christmas Magic and I stand before him now."

All eyes turned to Ismus as a radiant light appeared around him. A warm sensation washed over him as he knelt on one knee gazing up into a celestial light that enveloped him. He possessed the look of one who was listening intently to words that only he could hear. The pristine light with speckles of winter dust and snowflakes glistened upon his face.

"You have served the Light well," Tinsel said. "Your deeds of kindness inspire hope in others. You champion the cause of the poor, the different, and the outcast. For in you

resides the heart of Christmas. Your given name is Nicholas but you shall be known henceforth as Santa Claus. Father Christmas has decreed that you shall bear the Scepter of Christmas Magic. You and your merry band of Christmas companions will travel at dawn to the North Lands. Upon reaching Christmas Mountain, you will use the Scepter of Christmas to create the magical Kingdom of Christmas. In time, your exploits will become legends and inspire many hearts to soar with Christmas hope."

A silver scepter materialized in Tinsel's hand shaped like a shepherd's crook, possessing a magical stone that illumined in the starlight. The song of angels could be heard as a single shaft of starlight beamed down upon Santa Claus. Tinsel gently touched him on the head with the scepter as energy went forth through his body. Magically appearing threads covered his body in colors of red, white, silver, and black. Black boots covered his feet completing his transfiguration.

"You are the keeper of the Scepter of Christmas. Go forth to spread the magic of Christmas," Tinsel said as she blew upon him the spirit breath of Father Christmas. "Arise now Santa Claus, the Gift-bringer."

Santa Claus arose with the most jolly expression on his face. Turning to look around at his merry band of Christmas companions and all the rest of the villagers, he belted out his first words as Santa, "Merry Christmas! Merry Christmas to all!"

The villagers erupted in merry laughter and joyous acclaim. And Santa's first act as the paragon of Christmas would be to the little village girl he had met prior to leaving for the Dark Lands. Walking over to the little girl, Santa stooped down and said, "Tala, it is good to see you again. I have a gift for you."

"For me?!" sweet Tala beamed.

"Yes, for you!" Santa smiled. Turning to Derya, Santa signaled for her to bring

Tala's gift. Stepping out from behind Derya was Tala's brother. A fire of excitement ignited in her eyes as she rushed to give her brother a hug. The two held each other in a lingering embrace. After a time, Tala finally let go and then ran over to Santa giving him an endearing hug. "Thank you Santa! You gave me the best gift ever!"

"Ho! Ho! Ho!" Santa said returning Tala's loving embrace. "All good gifts come from above. Father Christmas smiles upon you dear child." Santa watched with beaming joy as Tala and her brother ran off together to play by the Christmas tree.

The Christmas angels lining Merry Mountain began glowing brighter as they slowly ascended toward the clear, bright stars above. "Blessed are the Imaginative Ones!" an angelic voice proclaimed, while ascending toward the stars. "And blessed are the dreamers!" another angelic voice added. Dash watched in awe as the Christmas angels vanished into the starlight.

Abominus the donkey began braying trying to communicate something. "And as for you," Tinsel said. "You have been very naughty, for fear is a terrible master. You bullied and banished others for being different. But we shall not be so callous in our treatment of you."

Tinsel signaled to Dunder and Rudimas who stepped forward. "Take Abominus and his sons to the stable where they shall spend Christmas finding solace in knowing that the Christ Child accepted and embraced the most lowly among us. And so to reject others who are different, is to reject the very Spirit of Christmas. A season in the hide of a donkey will teach you much about the true nature of humility. Learn well."

After watching Abominus the donkey and his two goat sons braying and bleating as they were lead toward the stable, Tinsel leaned over and whispered to Dash, "Someone wishes to see you."

"Who?" Dash asked.

"Someone very special," Tinsel said smiling.

Dash then felt his feet leave the ground as Tinsel took his hand and flew him over to the glowing tomb. Upon touching down, Dash immediately recognized one of the silhouetted figures standing next to a Christmas angel. "Dad," he shouted with excitement. Running over he leapt into his Dad's arms. "I knew I would see you again!"

"Dash, my son!" His Dad exclaimed while holding him in an affectionate embrace. Looking over Dash's shoulder at Tinsel he mouthed, "Thank you!"

"I am so very proud of you Dash," his Dad said. "Your courage and heroics are an inspiration to all." Dash just clung even tighter to his Dad as a tear trickled down his face.

Dash and his Dad spent time together walking the beach and tossing pebbles into the Great Sea as the stars above were twinkling in glorious splendor, refracting off the water. It was a magical time for Dash and a memory he would cherish forever.

Tinsel flew over with the other Christmas angel landing next to them both. "It is time," Tinsel said.

Dash turned and looked at his Dad, "Can my Dad come with us?" He asked imploringly.

His Dad wrapped his arms around Dash, "Dash, of course I will return with you, just in a different way. Sort of like Santa over there. Although he has a new name and looks different, Ismus is still forever a part of him. And so it is with us. We will always be together, just in a different way. My journey in this world has run its course. But yours is just beginning. Run well my son. It is, after all, the reason I nicknamed you Dash," his Dad said with a smile.

"I love you Dad!" Dash said feeling Christmas hope swelling in him.

"I love you too, son!" And with that his Dad soared alongside his accompanying angel back to the heavens above.

"He now lives in the place where Christmas reigns eternal," Santa said walking up and placing a hand on Dash's shoulder. "You will see him again in time. In the meantime my friend, you must return to your home and help me spread Christmas hope to all!" Santa said, with a reassuring smile. "But first things first. Let us celebrate Christmas together here on Merry Hill!"

Noticing Santa's scepter glowing, Dash was mesmerized by its magical appearance. "Here, you can hold it," Santa said observing Dash's keen interest in the Scepter of Christmas magic.

Santa handed the scepter to Dash who ran his fingers down the length of the ancient scepter. His eyes like refracting glass, began shimmering in hues of silver and blue, trailing down the shaft of the staff taking in the look and feel of the ancient scepter. He felt the smoothness of the sleek, silvery staff. Dash gazed in fascination at the scepter which possessed the similar shape of a numerical 9 at the top.

"It was originally a shepherd's staff, one of the sacred symbols of Christmas," Santa said. "It first belonged to a very special shepherd boy who visited the Christ Child on the night of his birth. The staff was infused with Christmas magic and transformed into a magical scepter when it was touched by the infant finger of the Christ Child. I met the young shepherd on my first Christmas adventure with Tinsel."

Dash was simply awestruck by the ancient symbol of Christmas. "Did the shepherd boy also hear the whispering wind?" Dash asked with growing interest.

"Boy did he ever!" Santa exclaimed with a jolly voice. "He was the first to see the Bethlehem star and to hear Tinsel's voice. And oh, how he fended off bandits and wolves with nothing but his staff and a drum. It was his gift of selfless service that inspired the Christ Child's brightest smile on that first blessed Christmas morn. His adventure is a big part of the first Christmas story written in Tinsel's book of Christmas magic."

"I see you are admiring the ancient shepherd's staff. Now that is a story worth telling," Tinsel winked knowingly at Santa.

"Can you tell me the story now?" Dash asked, eager to hear the recounting of the Christmas tale.

"Some tales are better experienced than heard," Santa said.

"How is this possible? Dash asked.

"All things are possible with a little faith and Christmas magic," Santa replied with a wink. "Besides, we are in the midst of intersecting stories as we speak, thanks to Tinsel."

"Come and let's make merry together as we celebrate this Christmas with story, song, and dance," Friar Nicholas hollered standing over by a campfire. "It shall be a celebration that none shall soon forget!"

"Come," Santa said. "Let us enjoy the rest of our story together and join in the Christmas celebration!"

Chapter 22

A MERRY CHRISTMAS

RIBBONS OF FLAME danced in firelight as multiple campfires burned brightly beneath the stars all a-glitter in their heavenly finery. Sounds of crackling fires, the feet of children playing on powdery snow, and chattering villagers filled the air with mirth excitement. Dash was staring into the fire, enjoying its lambent light, when a delicious thought excited him.

"What's got you all smiles?" Tinsel said observing his preoccupation with the dancing flames.

"I've got an idea and hoping you can help me with it," Dash said before leaning over and whispering into Tinsel's ear.

"I can do that," she twinkled merrily. With a flick of her hand, silver stardust scattered in the air encircling ribbons of flame dancing within the campfire. The glittering stardust vanished as marshmallows on sticks materialized jutting out of the ground creating a ring around the campfire.

Dash excitedly pulled a marshmallow stick out of the ground placing the soft, white marshmallow over licking flames. "You will love roasted marshmallows," Dash said eagerly, glancing over at Santa.

Santa and the others picked up a marshmallow stick and followed Dash's lead

placing the puffy, sugary treats over the spit. Dash pulled his treat-on-a-stick out of the flames and began blowing hard to cool the flaming white sponge of gooey deliciousness. Taking a bite, he smiled in sweet satisfaction.

"Ho! Ho! Ho!" Santa said taking a nibble from his dripping marshmallow, marveling at the delicious taste. "Now this is truly a Christmas delight!"

"Wait till you try it covered in chocolate," Dash said with a mouthful of marshmallow. "They're the best!"

"I shall look forward to such a treat," Santa said before taking another nibble.

Never one to lack for imagination, Derya walked over and whispered something in Tinsel's ear. "Now that is a great idea!" Tinsel beamed excitedly. "Let me see." Tinsel's angelic wings sprung to life with celestial energy as she whirred above the ground spinning several times before touching down as a burlap sack magically appeared over her shoulder, filled with red and white striped candy canes. "You can hand them out," Tinsel said giving Derya a wink. Making her way excitedly around the campfires on Merry Hill, Derya began handing out the candy canes to the delight of all.

Friar Nicholas appraised approvingly the candy cane in his hand which resembled the shape of a shepherd's staff. "A blessed treat. A blessed treat indeed," Friar Nicholas said as the smell of peppermint lingered in the air. Placing the long cylinder of mint-flavored candy in his mouth, he cackled in delight, "Ohhh! This is a glorious treat worthy of the angels!"

After a time of revelry and enjoyment, Santa and Derya, along with her helpers, unpacked burlap sacks from the sleigh carrying them over the Christmas tree. Santa removed an assortment of gifts that the Imaginative Ones had made while in the Dark Lands.

Children lined up at his invitation and one by one stepped forward to receive a gift from Santa. Smiles filled the faces of the villagers as they expressed their appreciation and gratitude by giving hugs to Santa, Derya and her imaginative helpers.

The hearts, hollow from despair, were now brimming with Christmas hope and joy. Friar Nicholas marveled at the sight before him, as gifts fashioned by gifted hands, warmed hearts and stirred imaginations. Long had he prayed to live to see the miracle of Christmas unfolding before him that was awakening the soul of the village. And now he knew that his ardent prayers had soared in winged wonder having returned with the blessed gifts of peace, hope, and joy.

Tinsel asked each of Santa's merry band of Christmas companions to step forward: Dunder, Rudimas, Dashire, Coamé, Cubyt, Blizha, Vixie-Rae, Dansar, and Praniel. "True strength comes from courage to act on behalf of those unable to defend themselves. Each of you exemplify the spirit of Christmas in that you risked your safety and comfort on behalf of those were teased, bullied, and shunned. And in so doing, you gave to the Imaginative Ones, priceless gifts of hope and friendship. Your compassion, bravery, and courage is an example for all to aspire. In recognition of such kind hearts, receive now the highest heavenly award given by a Christmas Angel – The Christmas Medallion of Valor." Tinsel then placed around the upper arm of each, a shimmering band made of silver stardust with a constellation blue moonstone encasing swirling blue fire within a medallion.

Turning to Derya and the Imaginative Ones, Tinsel beamed with admiration as she called them to stand before her. "Each of you have been gifted by the Creator. Wield your imagination and harness the power of dreams. Receive now the Spirit breath of Christmas," Tinsel said as she blew forth winter dust that swirled about them, transfiguring them into Christmas Elves. "You will join Santa as his helpers and with your imaginative and creative gifts, shall spread the Spirit of Christmas around the world."

Friar Nicholas gathered everybody around a roaring campfire. Many sat and stared in stared in wide-eyed wonder at the Christmas Elves adorned in colorful outfits of red, yellow, green, and blue. Others gazed up at Tinsel who sat perched atop the luminous Christmas tree as the moonstones shimmered in brilliance.

Friar Nicholas quickly captured the imaginations of all with a story about the birth of the Christ Child. It was a story about the birth of hope. And so too, the rise of Santa and his Christmas Elves was the birth of something new and wonderful that would inspire and transform the world with Christmas hope. Well into the starry night, stories were told and sung, enlarging imaginations and lifting spirits to the heavens.

Music filled the air with sounds of the Lyre, Pan-pipe, and Kithara. Many danced around the Christmas tree as the moonstones shimmered in a sparkling dance with the starlight. It was a most magical time on Merry Hill.

Friar Nicholas and Dunder spun round and round, arms interlocked while kicking up their heels to the joyful sounds.

Rudimas and Coamé with intertwined arms spun round and round, throwing their heads back while giving themselves over to the merriment that filled their hearts.

Blizha and Vixie-Rae joined hands as they skipped around a campfire in a starry Christmas bop, stomping their feet to the ground ever so often, creating a dance that looked like a couple of reindeer locking antlers while spinning round and round.

Cubyt grabbed Santa's hand and gave him a twirl around the Christmas tree as they both cackled and two-stepped to their own version of a do-si-do.

Dansar and Praniel hipped and hopped as one to the rhythm of the night performing flips, somersaults, and spins to the delight of all.

Tinsel swooped down and grabbed Dash's hand sweeping him up in the air as they twirled and danced above the Christmas tree. "Now this is Christdancing," Dash shouted with glee. It was a festive time for all, but none more so than for Dash.

"I never want to leave this place," Dash said. "Nor do I," Tinsel replied. After a lingering moment, Tinsel said, "But we must. Santa Claus will soon journey to the North Lands and you back to the South Lands."

Touching back down on the ground, Dash knelt down and began arranging marshmallows on the ground forming a perfectly shaped numerical 9. Not wanting to return home he wished to stay forever on Merry Hill with Santa and his merry band of Christmas companions.

"What is that you're creating there my merry friend?" Santa asked stooping down next to Dash.

"It's a 9," Dash said placing his marshmallow stick in the circle of the 9. "That is where you, my Dad, and all my friends here on Merry Hill are. And this," Dash said pointing to the tail of the 9, "is where I must go."

"Ah, the circle of the 9," Santa said, musing out loud.

"Do you know it?" Dash asked.

"Do I know it?! Why of course I know it. It came to me in a dream the night before you arrived. A young boy would come from afar and help lead the Different Ones out of the Dark Lands," Santa said while pointing his marshmallow stick at the circle of the 9, "and back to Merry Abbey." Santa finished saying while tracing his stick in the dirt along the tail of the 9.

Dash looked at Santa with bewilderment. He had never considered that the tail of the 9 could be as important as the circle of the 9.

"Dash," Santa said. "There are many outside the circle of the 9 who are counting on us to make a difference in their life. The Spirit of Christmas emanates from within the circle of the 9, but leads by the tail of the 9 to bring Christmas hope to others."

A revelation of understanding washed over Dash as he looked with eyes of new understanding at the 9 he had drawn in the dirt.

"We will meet again young one, and very soon," Santa said rising to his feet.

A tear trickled down Dash's face as he gazed into Santa's sparkling blue eyes. "Now, now, there my young friend. Don't you cry because I'm gonna tell you why," Santa said directing Dash's attention up toward the brilliant stars shining overhead. "When you hear the whispering wind and see Tinsel's star shining bright in the heavens, you will know that my arrival is near. So get ready. Go now and return to your home. Tell one, tell all! That Santa Claus is coming to town!" Santa exclaimed belting the most jolly, "Ho! Ho! Ho!"

Dash burst forth in laughter along with Tinsel. It was a good laugh.

Reaching out, Tinsel took Dash's hand as they began their ascent toward the heavens. Dash waved goodbye to Santa who was throwing a pebble out into the Great Sea. The pebble skipped along creating the most magical water splash as a 9 shimmered over the surface before racing up and past Dash.

The campfires on Merry Hill were like stars twinkling from the ground below. It was as if Dash's world had been turned upside down again but only this time he longed to be back down among those dancing stars below. Merry Abbey encompassed the circle of the 9 and the train of camp fires along Merry Hill formed the tail of the 9. Standing along the tail of the 9 was Santa, Derya and the others waving goodbye to him. The memory of their magical adventure evoked a smile. Tinsel gave him a wink as they picked up speed.

Dash's eyes sparkled with joy as he recalled his Dad's words, "You're going to touch the stars. Just you wait and see." And his Dad was right. For he was holding the hand of the star that shines brightest on Christmas Eve. Closing his eyes, Dash gave himself over to the Christmas magic as the serenity of the whispering wind gently kissed his face.

Chapter 23

THE RETURN

LAYERS OF TIME peeled away, as Dash and Tinsel hurtled forward into the future, revealing snapshot glimpses of: a constellation resembling a reindeer, red and white steaks of light, campfires littering a mountain side more numerous than the stars, and the intermittent sounds of caroling. Dash was witnessing in real time centuries of Christmases past accelerating in rapid succession toward Christmas future.

The stream of time raced by creating a blue and white tunnel effect with snow and stardust whirling all around. Fascinated by the ethereal beauty of the time tunnel, Dash reached out his hand to touch the snow and stardust particles, enjoying the cool tingling sensations that charged through his body.

"Can we slow down?" Dash asked desiring to delay the return.

"We most certainly can," Tinsel replied bringing them to a slow crawl within the time tunnel. Through the thin sheen of blue and white orbing energy, Dash saw a castle below on a very large hill with torches lit upon several turrets. The land around the castle was eerily shrouded in darkness. "It is so dark down there. When are we in time?" Dash asked.

"Oh my," Tinsel said. "A dark time. A very dark time indeed."

"Does the sun ever come out?" Dash asked taking her literally.

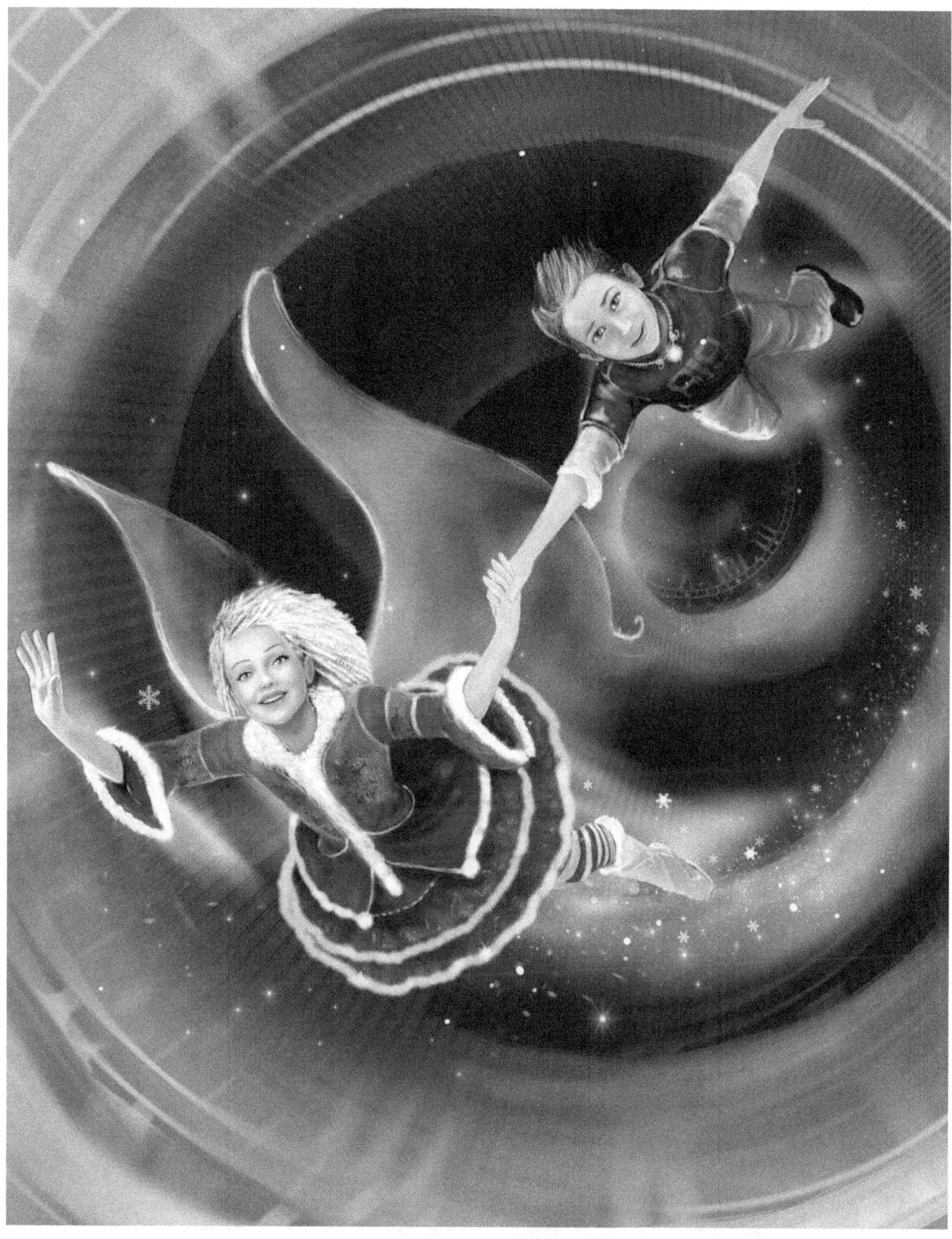

"Yes, but I speak of a different kind of darkness. We now gaze through the veil of time having arrived at the height of the Dark Ages, when many of those who looked and thought differently were vilified. They were accused of being wicked witches and shameful sorcerers, friends of fiends, and companions of goblins, sprites, and trolls. And as you can well imagine, not all was as it seemed," Tinsel said as Dash shuddered at her words.

"You mean there were people like Abominus and his bullying sons? Dash asked anxiously.

"I'm afraid so. But there were also people like Ismus and his merry band of Christmas companions. *The Book of Christmas Magic* would have been lost forever if not for a young girl, not much older than yourself, who pierced the darkness with the light of Christmas that burned strong in her; as it does in you," Tinsel said with an admiring smile. "But her adventures will be joined by the journey of one whose deeds are yet to be recorded in *The Book of Christmas Magic.*"

"But if we are hovering in the past, then how can her adventures not yet be recorded, if we are soaring in time to Christmas future?" Dash asked, perplexed and confused by the paradox.

"Her tale awaits the one from Christmas future chosen to accompany her. Choices will be made, allegiances forged, and mysteries revealed. Only when one's adventure has been completed, will the story be written within the pages of *The Book of Christmas Magic,*" Tinsel said knowingly.

Dash struggled to comprehend the seemingly enigmatic words before he a ray of insight crossed his mind. "Tinsel time!" Dash exclaimed excitedly. "*The Book of Christmas Magic* goes by Tinsel time."

"I love it," Tinsel said placing her arm around Dash's shoulder. "Come now, I've got to get you back in time for Santa's arrival."

"Really?!" Dash asked eagerly. "Santa's coming to Charleston?"

"Now, what do you think?" Tinsel replied with a grin, before spinning around in glee as stardust and snowflakes cascaded all around. "Yes! Santa Claus is coming to town!"

"Let's get home," Dash said with eyes aglow in starlight. "I've got to get ready!"

"You bet you do. Your adventure isn't over yet!" Tinsel exclaimed. "Now, hold on!" And off they soared, rushing ever closer toward the moment in time when Tinsel and Dash departed on Christmas Eve.

Chapter 24

UNDER THE STARS

ASH HIT THE ground running before pulling up sharp, noticing the 9 starfish on the sand just as he last saw them. It was as if time had stood still awaiting his return before continuing its ticktock cadence.

Hearing the faint sounds of Christmas carols off in the distance, Dash excitedly said to Tinsel, "It's still Christmas Eve!

"Yes it is," Tinsel replied as her wings whirred with astral energy.

"Dash! It's time to come in," his mom called out from the porch of their beachfront home.

"I've got to get everything ready in time for Santa's arrival," Dash said to Tinsel.

"Yes, you better," Tinsel said with a giggle. "For if I know Santa Claus, he is on his way, heading straight for your home with his merry band of Christmas companions out front of that magical sleigh."

"I've got to hurry," Dash said with a plan forming in his mind.

"Well, don't let me keep you waiting," Tinsel said twirling about excitedly in the air, sending forth snowflakes cascading all around. Dash ran as fast as he could, losing no time unlatching the gate of a white picket fence before racing across the yard and up the porch steps. Opening the door he exclaimed uncharacteristically, "Mom, I've got

to get the lights on the Christmas tree!"

"Dash, whatever are you talking about? The Christmas tree already has lights on it," his Mom said, looking over at the Christmas tree aglow in the window illumined by white lights.

"No, not that tree. The one outside. Santa is on his way and I must quickly decorate the Palmetto tree outside," Dash said hurriedly.

"But I thought you wanted me to have the palmetto tree removed," his Mom replied, somewhat bewildered by Dash's change of heart.

In hopes of bringing him some measure of comfort, his Mom had the palmetto tree planted in in memory of his Dad. But the palmetto tree was only a reminder to Dash of all that was out of sorts within the circle of the 9. But all that had changed, thanks to Tinsel.

"No! The palmetto tree is right where it's supposed to be," Dash hollered back from down the hallway. Running to his closet, Dash immediately saw what he was looking for, a box neatly tucked away in the far corner. Dragging the box out, he opened it and removed a special strand of multicolored lights that he and his Dad always placed on the Christmas tree. Hurriedly, he rushed to the garage and grabbed a ladder and extension cord.

Dash's Mom marveled at the change that had come over Dash, as he scurried outside to decorate the palmetto tree. "Would you like some help?" She called out.

"No," Dash answered emphatically. "Everything has to be placed precisely on the tree."

"Ok," she said. "Don't be too long!"

Climbing the ladder, Dash busied himself with placing the colored lights on the palmetto tree. Satisfied that the lights were arrayed properly, Dash quickly climbed back down the ladder to connect the lights to an extension cord. Running back to the house,

Dash grabbed a sleeping bag.

"Where are you going with that?" his Mom asked.

"I'm sleeping under the stars tonight by the palmetto tree," Dash replied.

"Under the stars?" his Mom asked.

"Yes. Santa, is coming to town, so I want to be waiting when he arrives! He really likes a Christmas tree decorated under the stars," Dash said, rushing out the door.

"Okay, but only till he arrives and then you come inside," his Mom hollered as Dash was already exiting the white picket gate.

Dash placed his sleeping bag on the ground, but didn't turn around to look at the colored lights illuminating his yard. No, he need to first be standing in very special spot. Walking over to the 9 starfish, he took his place within the circle of the 9. Feeling the soft ocean breeze on his face he whispered, "Christmas hope soars in the heart." Turning slowly toward the palm tree, his eyes gleamed like brilliant starlight.

The palmetto tree had been transformed into a Christmas tree, cast in vivid colors of blue, green, red, white, purple, orange, pink, gold, and silver; nine colors forming a perfect number 9. Serving as a beacon, the luminescent 9 would easily be seen by Santa from above. But there was something missing at the top of the Christmas tree. Dash's heart started beating faster as he frantically looked around.

"What an amazing Christmas tree," Tinsel said, easing his growing anxiety.

"I thought you had left," Dash replied.

"Leave without saying Merry Christmas?" Tinsel said, placing her hands on her hips with a raised eyebrow.

In the distance, Dash heard the first of the twelve chimes of the bell from a church, announcing the arrival of Christmas. Dash gazed to the heavens, scanning every twinkle and sign of movement hoping to spot Santa Claus.

"Isn't the Great Sea over there?" Dash asked pointing out over the Atlantic Ocean.

"It certainly is but a little more to the right," Tinsel said alighting on the ground next to him.

"Do you see him yet?" Dash asked in great expectation, keeping his eyes fixed on the infinite horizon.

"Oh, you bet I do," Tinsel answered.

"Where?" Dash asked, eyes fixed on the starry heavens before noticing a perfect alignment of stars forming a numerical 9. And within the circle of the constellation of 9, there was movement.

Hearing the distinct sounds of jingle bells, faint at first, and then becoming louder, Dash made out a faint red and white glow moving across the skyline. "It's Santa Claus!" Dash yelled with glee. "And he's coming to town!"

Chapter 25

THE GIFT

AIR WHOOSHED PAST Dash, as Santa Claus swooped by in a red sleigh trailing nine reindeer out front. A sparkling red chariot with silver bells ringing along the edges streaked around the curve of the island as Santa positioned the sleigh for a final approach. He held the reins loosely as the reindeer hit the soft sands running before bringing the sleigh to a stop directly in front of Dash.

"Ho! Ho! Ho! Merry Christmas!" Santa Claus called out merrily.

Dash ran up and gave Santa the biggest hug wrapping his arms as far as they would go around Santa's waist. "I knew you would come," Dash said clinging tightly.

"And I knew you would be waiting," Santa said returning Dash's hug with a warm embrace of his own. "I've been looking forward to telling you how much I've been enjoying a delicious diet of marshmallows and candy canes," Santa said with a wry grin. "You were right about the chocolate covered marshmallows. They are Christmalicious!"

"Did Derya make you a new sleigh?" Dash asked, admiring Santa's sleigh.

"This is a gift from Father Christmas. Much has happened since we saw each other," Santa replied with the glint of adventure in his eye.

"Where is Rudimas and the others?" Dash asked.

"They are back at the North Pole enjoying a little rest and relaxation," Santa replied.

Just then something stirred in the back of the sleigh catching Dash's attention. Emerging from behind a large red sack filled with toys, Derya popped out and leapt down from the sleigh. Wearing a silver vest that glittered in the starlight, Derya carried a gift wrapped in red and white with a silver bow.

"Merry Christmas," Derya said.

"Derya," Dash said giving her a hug before stepping back quickly feeling a little embarrassed.

"I'm happy to see you also," Derya said smiling happily. "I have been looking forward to traveling to these here South Lands and to bring you a very special gift."

Dash's eyes lit up in delight like a Christmas tree at the sight of the gift. Meticulously he opened it, so as not to tear up the silver package with a sapphire blue bow. He was already imagining a place in his special memory box, back in his closet where he would keep it along with all things near and dear to his heart.

Removing the gift, a dazzling star-shaped moonstone illumined as his eyes refracted the brilliant blue light. Dash's heart leapt in glee as he grinned from ear to ear. "Derya helped me to shape and polish the moonstone for you," Santa said. "It too, is one of the sacred symbols of Christmas. For the Angel star guides us on our life journey, her light ever illumining the heart with Christmas hope."

"Thank you, Santa! I will take good care of it and cherish it always," Dash said with a thankful heart.

"I know you will," Santa replied. "And in so doing, you will discover that it will take good care of you as well."

Gazing at the star, Dash was fascinated by its illumination emanating from Tinsel's light shining down from atop the Christmas tree.

"I must go now," Santa said stirring Dash from his preoccupying thoughts.

"Will I see you again?" Dash asked, wrapping his arms around Santa as his eyes began watering over.

"Can Reindeer fly?" Santa replied with a jolly smile.

"Yes," Dash answered with a chuckle.

"Our adventure together is one that I will forever cherish in my heart, " Santa said admiringly. "Till we meet again, you keep Christmas hope soaring in your heart."

"Merry Christmas Santa," Dash said, giving a lingering hug.

"And a Merry Christmas to you as well my young friend," Santa said, returning Dash's hug.

Santa stepped onto his sleigh and paused to gaze up at Tinsel who was beaming like a star, from atop the Christmas tree. "Merry Christmas, bright one! You are a child's greatest gift."

"And a Merry Christmas to you dear friend," Tinsel replied.

Tinsel gave Santa a wink as he sounded out the names of his reindeer before giving the command, "Now soar away! Soar away all!"

Dash ran down the beach chasing after Santa's sleigh as Derya waved from the back before the sleigh gained lift, dashing away like a shooting star across the sky. "Christmas hope soars in the heart," Dash called out as they quickly vanished from sight.

Walking back over to the 9 starfish, Dash gazed down as a smile spread across his lips. His world within the circle of 9 gleamed brightly. Not wanting the night to ever end, he clung to the memory of the special Christmas Eve adventure that he shared with Tinsel and Santa Claus. It was the truest and best gift ever.

Dash and Tinsel sat beneath the stars and shared together a great many things before Dash finally drifted off soundly asleep beneath the constellation of the 9. The star-shaped moonstone gleamed next to him. "Christmas hope soars in your heart. The most powerful magic of all," Tinsel said, with a wink from atop the Christmas tree.

The book of Christmas magic opened as the silver strand of tinsel formed the tip of a quill pen and began writing the story of Dash's journey within the sacred pages. The book of Christmas magic closed before slowly rising up from the sand and began to whirl round and round the Christmas tree with snowflakes and stardust bursting forth. Slowly, it ascended toward the top of the Christmas tree where Tinsel sat perched.

Tinsel and the magical book coalesced in essence forming a brilliant star before soaring to the heavens above. The brilliance of Tinsel's star made the other stars shine a little brighter. She winked one last time before receding among the starry heavens where she awaits to reappear for another magical adventure, next Christmas Eve.

Thus ends the tale of Tinsel and Dash and the grand adventure they shared. One that restored balance and hope to Dash's unsettled world. An adventure that teaches us, as it did Dash, that imagination is part inspiration and part desperation. For when Christmas hope soars in the heart, all things are possible. Dash called this Christmas hope, "Tinsel's magic". And what Christmas magic it was.

The End

The Adventure Continues

Experience The Magic That Changed The World

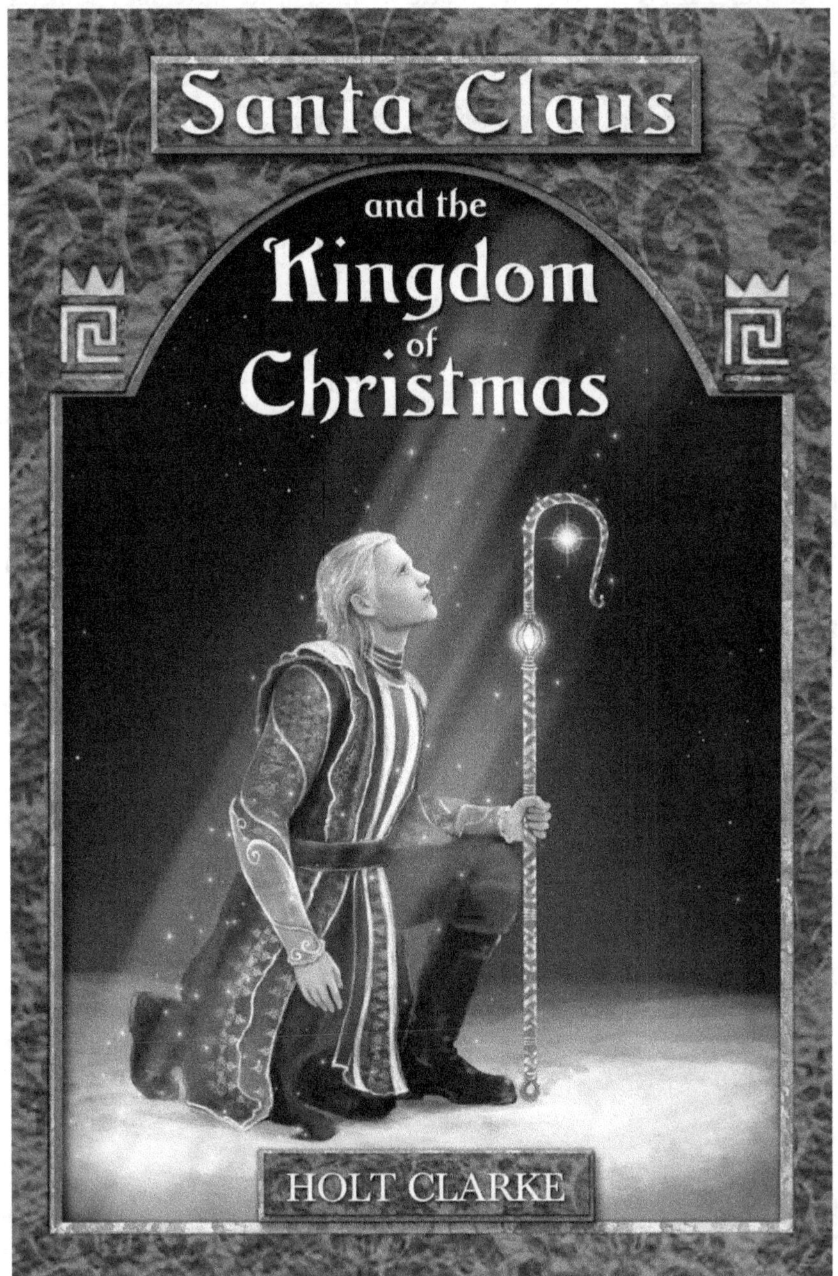

For more information visit HoltClarke.com

OTHER BOOKS BY HOLT CLARKE

ABOUT THE AUTHOR

Holt Clarke is the father of the coolest kids on earth, on Santa's Nice List, livin' the dream, and keep'n the magic real in Charleston, South Carolina.

Holt earned the Doctor of Ministry degree from Drew University, Master of Divinity degree from Duke University, and Bachelor of Arts degree from North Carolina Wesleyan College.

Visit his website @ www.HoltClarke.com

Connect on Social Media:
www.facebook.com/holtaclarke
www.twitter.com/holtaclarke

Like Tinsel @ www.facebook.com/TinselandtheBookofChristmasMagic

www.ingramcontent.com/pod-product-compliance
Lightning Source LLC
Chambersburg PA
CBHW082102090726

47910CB00008B/2559